CABIN FEVER

LECTOR HOUSE PUBLIC DOMAIN WORKS

CABIN FEVER

B. M. BOWER

ISBN: 978-93-5342-378-0

First Published: -

© LECTOR HOUSE LLP

LECTOR HOUSE LLP
E-MAIL: lectorpublishing@gmail.com

CABIN FEVER

BY

B. M. BOWER

CONTENTS

CABIN FEVER

CHAPTER ONE.

THE FEVER MANIFESTS ITSELF

There is a certain malady of the mind induced by too much of one thing. Just as the body fed too long upon meat becomes a prey to that horrid disease called scurvy, so the mind fed too long upon monotony succumbs to the insidious mental ailment which the West calls "cabin fever." True, it parades under different names, according to circumstances and caste. You may be afflicted in a palace and call it ennui, and it may drive you to commit peccadillos and indiscretions of various sorts. You may be attacked in a middle-class apartment house, and call it various names, and it may drive you to cafe life and affinities and alimony. You may have it wherever you are shunted into a backwater of life, and lose the sense of being borne along in the full current of progress. Be sure that it will make you abnormally sensitive to little things; irritable where once you were amiable; glum where once you went whistling about your work and your play. It is the crystallizer of character, the acid test of friendship, the final seal set upon enmity. It will betray your little, hidden weaknesses, cut and polish your undiscovered virtues, reveal you in all your glory or your vileness to your companions in exile—if so be you have any.

If you would test the soul of a friend, take him into the wilderness and rub elbows with him for five months! One of three things will surely happen: You will hate each other afterward with that enlightened hatred which is seasoned with contempt; you will emerge with the contempt tinged with a pitying toleration, or you will be close, unquestioning friends to the last six feet of earth—and beyond. All these things will cabin fever do, and more. It has committed murder, many's the time. It has driven men crazy. It has warped and distorted character out of all semblance to its former self. It has sweetened love and killed love. There is an antidote—but I am going to let you find the antidote somewhere in the story.

Bud Moore, ex-cow-puncher and now owner of an auto stage that did not run in the winter, was touched with cabin fever and did not know what ailed him. His stage line ran from San Jose up through Los Gatos and over the Bear Creek road across the summit of the Santa Cruz Mountains and down to the State Park, which is locally called Big Basin. For something over fifty miles of wonderful scenic travel he charged six dollars, and usually his big car was loaded to the running boards. Bud was a good driver, and he had a friendly pair of eyes—dark blue and with a humorous little twinkle deep down in them somewhere—and a human little smiley quirk at the corners of his lips. He did not know it, but these things helped to fill his car.

Until gasoline married into the skylark family, Bud did well enough to keep him contented out of a stock saddle. (You may not know it, but it is harder for an old cow-puncher to find content, now that the free range is gone into history, than it is for a labor agitator to be happy in a municipal boarding house.)

Bud did well enough, which was very well indeed. Before the second season closed with the first fall rains, he had paid for his big car and got the insurance policy transferred to his name. He walked up First Street with his hat pushed back and a cigarette dangling from the quirkiest corner of his mouth, and his hands in his pockets. The glow of prosperity warmed his manner toward the world. He had a little money in the bank, he had his big car, he had the good will of a smiling world. He could not walk half a block in any one of three or four towns but he was hailed with a "Hello, Bud!" in a welcoming tone. More people knew him than Bud remembered well enough to call by name—which is the final proof of popularity the world over.

In that glowing mood he had met and married a girl who went into Big Basin with her mother and camped for three weeks. The girl had taken frequent trips to Boulder Creek, and twice had gone on to San Jose, and she had made it a point to ride with the driver because she was crazy about cars. So she said. Marie had all the effect of being a pretty girl. She habitually wore white middies with blue collar and tie, which went well with her clear, pink skin and her hair that just escaped being red. She knew how to tilt her "beach" hat at the most provocative angle, and she knew just when to let Bud catch a slow, sidelong glance—of the kind that is supposed to set a man's heart to syncopatic behavior. She did not do it too often. She did not powder too much, and she had the latest slang at her pink tongue's tip and was yet moderate in her use of it.

Bud did not notice Marie much on the first trip. She was demure, and Bud had a girl in San Jose who had brought him to that interesting stage of dalliance where he wondered if he dared kiss her good night the next time he called. He was preoccupiedly reviewing the she-said-and-then-I-said, and trying to make up his mind whether he should kiss her and take a chance on her displeasure, or whether he had better wait. To him Marie appeared hazily as another camper who helped fill the car—and his pocket—and was not at all hard to look at. It was not until the third trip that Bud thought her beautiful, and was secretly glad that he had not kissed that San Jose girl.

You know how these romances develop. Every summer is saturated with them the world over. But Bud happened to be a simple-souled fellow, and there was something about Marie—He didn't know what it was. Men never do know, until it is all over. He only knew that the drive through the shady stretches of woodland grew suddenly to seem like little journeys into paradise. Sentiment lurked behind every great, mossy tree bole. New beauties unfolded in the winding drive up over the mountain crests. Bud was terribly in love with the world in those days.

There were the evenings he spent in the Basin, sitting beside Marie in the huge campfire circle, made wonderful by the shadowy giants, the redwoods; talking foolishness in undertones while the crowd sang snatches of songs which no one knew from beginning to end, and that went very lumpy in the verses and very much out of harmony in the choruses. Sometimes they would stroll down toward that sweeter music the creek made, and stand beside one of the enormous trees and watch the glow of the fire, and the silhouettes of the people gathered around it.

In a week they were surreptitiously holding hands. In two weeks they could scarcely endure the partings when Bud must start back to San Jose, and were taxing their ingenuity to invent new reasons why Marie must go along. In three weeks they were married, and Marie's mother—a shrewd, shrewish widow—was trying to decide whether she should wash her hands of Marie, or whether it might be well to accept the situation and hope that Bud would prove himself a rising young man.

But that was a year in the past. Bud had cabin fever now and did not know what ailed him, though cause might have been summed up in two meaty phrases: too much idleness, and too much mother-in-law. Also, not enough comfort and not enough love.

In the kitchen of the little green cottage on North Sixth Street where Bud had built the home nest with much nearly-Mission furniture and a piano, Bud was frying his own hotcakes for his ten o'clock breakfast, and was scowling over the task. He did not mind the hour so much, but he did mortally hate to cook his own breakfast—or any other meal, for that matter. In the next room a rocking chair was rocking with a rhythmic squeak, and a baby was squalling with that sustained volume of sound which never fails to fill the adult listener with amazement. It affected Bud unpleasantly, just as the incessant bawling of a band of weaning calves used to do. He could not bear the thought of young things going hungry.

"For the love of Mike, Marie! Why don't you feed that kid, or do something to shut him up?" he exploded suddenly, dribbling pancake batter over the untidy range.

The squeak, squawk of the rocker ceased abruptly. "'Cause it isn't time yet to feed him—that's why. What's burning out there? I'll bet you've got the stove all over dough again—" The chair resumed its squeaking, the baby continued uninterrupted its wah-h-hah! wah-h-hah, as though it was a phonograph that had been wound up with that record on, and no one around to stop it

Bud turned his hotcakes with a vicious flop that spattered more batter on the stove. He had been a father only a month or so, but that was long enough to learn many things about babies which he had never known before. He knew, for instance, that the baby wanted its bottle, and that Marie was going to make him wait till feeding time by the clock.

"By heck, I wonder what would happen if that darn clock was to stop!" he exclaimed savagely, when his nerves would bear no more. "You'd let the kid starve to death before you'd let your own brains tell you what to do! Husky youngster like that—feeding 'im four ounces every four days—or some simp rule like that—" He lifted the cakes on to a plate that held two messy-looking fried eggs whose yolks had broken, set the plate on the cluttered table and slid petulantly into a chair and began to eat. The squeaking chair and the crying baby continued to torment him. Furthermore, the cakes were doughy in the middle.

"For gosh sake, Marie, give that kid his bottle!" Bud exploded again. "Use the brains God gave yuh—such as they are! By heck, I'll stick that darn book in the stove. Ain't yuh got any feelings at all? Why, I wouldn't let a dog go hungry like that! Don't yuh reckon the kid knows when he's hungry? Why, good Lord! I'll take and feed him myself, if you don't. I'll burn that book—so help me!"

"Yes, you will—not!" Marie's voice rose shrewishly, riding the high waves of the baby's incessant outcry against the restrictions upon appetite imposed by enlightened motherhood. "You do, and see what'll happen! You'd have him howling with colic, that's what you'd do."

"Well, I'll tell the world he wouldn't holler for grub! You'd go by the book if it told yuh to stand 'im on his head in the ice chest! By heck, between a woman and a hen turkey, give me the turkey when it comes to sense. They do take care of their young ones—"

"Aw, forget that! When it comes to sense—-"

Oh, well, why go into details? You all know how these domestic storms arise, and how love washes overboard when the matrimonial ship begins to wallow in the seas of recrimination.

Bud lost his temper and said a good many things should not have said. Marie flung back angry retorts and reminded Bud of all his sins and slights and short-comings, and told him many of mamma's pessimistic prophecies concerning him, most of which seemed likely to be fulfilled. Bud fought back, telling Marie how much of a snap she had had since she married him, and how he must have looked like ready money to her, and added that now, by heck, he even had to do his own cooking, as well as listen to her whining and nagging, and that there wasn't clean corner in the house, and she'd rather let her own baby go hungry than break a simp rule in a darn book got up by a bunch of boobs that didn't know anything about kids. Surely to goodness, he finished his heated paragraph, it wouldn't break any woman's back to pour a little warm water on a little malted milk, and shake it up.

He told Marie other things, and in return, Marie informed him that he was just a big-mouthed, lazy brute, and she could curse the day she ever met him. That was going pretty far. Bud reminded her that she had not done any cursing at the time, being in his opinion too busy roping him in to support her.

By that time he had gulped down his coffee, and was into his coat, and looking for his hat. Marie, crying and scolding and rocking the vociferous infant, interrupted herself to tell him that she wanted a ten-cent roll of cotton from the drug store, and added that she hoped she would not have to wait until next Christmas for it, either. Which bit of sarcasm so inflamed Bud's rage that he swore every step of the way to Santa Clara Avenue, and only stopped then because he happened to meet a friend who was going down town, and they walked together.

At the drug store on the corner of Second Street Bud stopped and bought the cotton, feeling remorseful for some of the things he had said to Marie, but not enough so to send him back home to tell her he was sorry. He went on, and met another friend before he had taken twenty steps. This friend was thinking of buying a certain second-hand automobile that was offered at a very low price, and he wanted Bud to go with him and look her over. Bud went, glad of the excuse to kill the rest of the forenoon.

They took the car out and drove to Schutzen Park and back. Bud opined that she didn't bark to suit him, and she had a knock in her cylinders that shouted of carbon. They ran her into the garage shop and went deep into her vitals, and because she jerked when Bud threw her into second, Bud suspected that her bevel gears had lost a tooth or two, and was eager to find out for sure.

Bill looked at his watch and suggested that they eat first before they got all over grease by monkeying with the rear end. So they went to the nearest restaurant and had smothered beefsteak and mashed potato and coffee and pie, and while they ate they talked of gears and carburetors and transmission and ignition troubles, all of which alleviated temporarily Bud's case of cabin fever and caused him to forget that he was married and had quarreled with his wife and had heard a good many unkind things which his mother-in-law had said about him.

By the time they were back in the garage and had the grease cleaned out of the rear gears so that they could see whether they were really burred or broken, as Bud had suspected, the twinkle was back in his eyes, and the smiley quirk stayed at the corners of his mouth, and when he was not talking mechanics with Bill he was whistling. He found much lost motion and four broken teeth, and he was grease to his eyebrows—in other words, he was happy.

When he and Bill finally shed their borrowed overalls and caps, the garage lights were on, and the lot behind the shop was dusky. Bud sat down on the running board and began to figure what the actual cost of the bargain would be when Bill had put it into good mechanical condition. New bearings, new bevel gear, new brake, lining, rebored cylinders—they totalled a sum that made Bill gasp.

By the time Bud had proved each item an absolute necessity, and had reached the final ejaculation: "Aw, forget it, Bill, and buy yuh a Ford!" it was so late that he knew Marie must have given up looking for him home to supper. She would have taken it for granted that he had eaten down town. So, not to disappoint her, Bud did eat down town. Then Bill wanted him to go to a movie, and after a praiseworthy hesitation Bud yielded to temptation and went. No use going home now, just when Marie would be rocking the kid to sleep and wouldn't let him speak above a whisper, he told his conscience. Might as well wait till they settled down for the night.

CHAPTER TWO.
TWO MAKE A QUARREL

At nine o'clock Bud went home. He was feeling very well satisfied with himself for some reason which he did not try to analyze, but which was undoubtedly his sense of having saved Bill from throwing away six hundred dollars on a bum car; and the weight in his coat pocket of a box of chocolates that he had bought for Marie. Poor girl, it was kinda tough on her, all right, being tied to the house now with the kid. Next spring when he started his run to Big Basin again, he would get a little camp in there by the Inn, and take her along with him when the travel wasn't too heavy. She could stay at either end of the run, just as she took a notion. Wouldn't hurt the kid a bit—he'd be bigger then, and the outdoors would make him grow like a pig. Thinking of these things, Bud walked briskly, whistling as he neared the little green house, so that Marie would know who it was, and would not be afraid when he stepped up on the front porch.

He stopped whistling rather abruptly when he reached the house, for it was dark. He tried the door and found it locked. The key was not in the letter box where they always kept it for the convenience of the first one who returned, so Bud went around to the back and climbed through the pantry window. He fell over a chair, bumped into the table, and damned a few things. The electric light was hung in the center of the room by a cord that kept him groping and clutching in the dark before he finally touched the elusive bulb with his fingers and switched on the light.

The table was set for a meal—but whether it was dinner or supper Bud could not determine. He went into the little sleeping room and turned on the light there, looked around the empty room, grunted, and tiptoed into the bedroom. (In the last month he had learned to enter on his toes, lest he waken the baby.) He might have saved himself the bother, for the baby was not there in its new gocart. The gocart was not there, Marie was not there—one after another these facts impressed themselves upon Bud's mind, even before he found the letter propped against the clock in the orthodox manner of announcing unexpected departures. Bud read the letter, crumpled it in his fist, and threw it toward the little heating stove. "If that's the way yuh feel about it, I'll tell the world you can go and be darned!" he snorted, and tried to let that end the matter so far as he was concerned. But he could not shake off the sense of having been badly used. He did not stop to consider that while he was working off his anger, that day, Marie had been rocking back and forth, crying and magnifying the quarrel as she dwelt upon it, and putting a new and sinister meaning into Bud's ill-considered utterances. By the time Bud was thinking only of the bargain car's hidden faults, Marie had reached the white heat of resentment that demanded vigorous action. Marie was packing a suitcase and meditating upon the scorching letter she meant to write.

Judging from the effect which the letter had upon Bud, it must have been a masterpiece of its kind. He threw the box of chocolates into the wood-box, crawled out of the window by which he had entered, and went down town to a hotel. If the house wasn't good enough for Marie, let her go. He could go just as fast and as far as she could. And if she thought he was going to hot-foot it over to her mother's and whine around and beg her to come home, she had another think coming.

He wouldn't go near the darn place again, except to get his clothes. He'd bust up the joint, by thunder. He'd sell off the furniture and turn the house over to the agent again, and Marie could whistle for a home. She had been darn glad to get into that house, he remembered, and away from that old cat of a mother. Let her stay there now till she was darn good and sick of it. He'd just keep her guessing for awhile; a week or so would do her good. Well, he wouldn't sell the furniture—he'd just move it into another house, and give her a darn good scare. He'd get a better one, that had a porcelain bathtub instead of a zinc one, and a better porch, where the kid could be out in the sun. Yes, sir, he'd just do that little thing, and lay low and see what Marie did about that. Keep her guessing—that was the play to make.

Unfortunately for his domestic happiness, Bud failed to take into account two very important factors in the quarrel. The first and most important one was Marie's mother, who, having been a widow for fifteen years and therefore having acquired a habit of managing affairs that even remotely concerned her, assumed that Marie's affairs must be managed also. The other factor was Marie's craving to be coaxed back to smiles by the man who drove her to tears. Marie wanted Bud to come and say he was sorry, and had been a brute and so forth. She wanted to hear him tell how empty the house had seemed when he returned and found her gone. She wanted him to be good and scared with that letter. She stayed awake until after midnight, listening for his anxious footsteps; after midnight she stayed awake to cry over the inhuman way he was treating her, and to wish she was dead, and so forth; also because the baby woke and wanted his bottle, and she was teaching him to sleep all night without it, and because the baby had a temper just like his father.

His father's temper would have yielded a point or two, the next day, had it been given the least encouragement. For instance, he might have gone over to see Marie before he moved the furniture out of the house, had he not discovered an express wagon standing in front of the door when he went home about noon to see if Marie had come back. Before he had recovered to the point of profane speech, the express man appeared, coming out of the house, bent nearly double under the weight of Marie's trunk. Behind him in the doorway Bud got a glimpse of Marie's mother.

That settled it. Bud turned around and hurried to the nearest drayage company, and ordered a domestic wrecking crew to the scene; in other words, a packer and two draymen and a dray. He'd show 'em. Marie and her mother couldn't put anything over on him—he'd stand over that furniture with a sheriff first.

He went back and found Marie's mother still there, packing dishes and doilies and the like. They had a terrible row, and all the nearest neighbors inclined ears to doors ajar—getting an earful, as Bud contemptuously put it. He finally led Marie's mother to the front door and set her firmly outside. Told her that Marie had come to him with no more than the clothes she had, and that his money had bought every teaspoon and every towel and every stick of furniture in the darned place, and he'd be everlastingly thus-and-so if they were going to strong-arm the stuff off him now. If Marie was too good to live with him, why, his stuff was too good for her to have.

Oh, yes, the neighbors certainly got an earful, as the town gossips proved when the divorce suit seeped into the papers. Bud refused to answer the proceedings, and was therefore ordered to pay twice as much alimony as he could afford to pay; more, in fact, than all his domestic expense had amounted to in the fourteen months that he had been married. Also Marie was awarded the custody of the child and, because Marie's mother had represented Bud to be a violent man who was a menace to her daughter's safety—and proved it by the neighbors who had seen and heard so much—Bud was served with a legal paper that wordily enjoined him from annoying Marie with his presence.

That unnecessary insult snapped the last thread of Bud's regret for what had happened. He sold the furniture and the automobile, took the money to the judge that had tried the case, told the judge a few wholesome truths, and laid the pile of money on the desk.

"That cleans me out, Judge," he said stolidly. "I wasn't such a bad husband, at that. I got sore—but I'll bet you get sore yourself and tell your wife what-for, now and then. I didn't get a square deal, but that's all right. I'm giving a better deal than I got. Now you can keep that money and pay it out to Marie as she needs it, for herself and the kid. But for the Lord's sake, Judge, don't let that wildcat of a mother of hers get her fingers into the pile! She framed this deal, thinking she'd get a haul outa me this way. I'm asking you to block that little game. I've held out ten dollars, to eat on till I strike something. I'm clean; they've licked the platter and broke the dish. So don't never ask me to dig up any more, because I won't—not for you nor no other darn man. Get that."

This, you must know, was not in the courtroom, so Bud was not fined for contempt. The judge was a married man himself, and he may have had a sympathetic understanding of Bud's position. At any rate he listened unofficially, and helped Bud out with the legal part of it, so that Bud walked out of the judge's office financially free, even though he had a suspicion that his freedom would not bear the test of prosperity, and that Marie's mother would let him alone only so long as he and prosperity were strangers.

CHAPTER THREE.

TEN DOLLARS AND A JOB FOR BUD

To withhold for his own start in life only one ten-dollar bill from fifteen hundred dollars was spectacular enough to soothe even so bruised an ego as Bud Moore carried into the judge's office. There is an anger which carries a person to the extreme of self-sacrifice, in the subconscious hope of exciting pity for one so hardly used. Bud was boiling with such an anger, and it demanded that he should all but give Marie the shirt off his back, since she had demanded so much—and for so slight a cause.

Bud could not see for the life of him why Marie should have quit for that little ruction. It was not their first quarrel, nor their worst; certainly he had not expected it to be their last. Why, he asked the high heavens, had she told him to bring home a roll of cotton, if she was going to leave him? Why had she turned her back on that little home, that had seemed to mean as much to her as it had to him?

Being kin to primitive man, Bud could only bellow rage when he should have analyzed calmly the situation. He should have seen that Marie too had cabin fever, induced by changing too suddenly from carefree girlhood to the ills and irks of wifehood and motherhood. He should have known that she had been for two months wholly dedicated to the small physical wants of their baby, and that if his nerves were fraying with watching that incessant servitude, her own must be close to the snapping point; had snapped, when dusk did not bring him home repentant.

But he did not know, and so he blamed Marie bitterly for the wreck of their home, and he flung down all his worldly goods before her, and marched off feeling self-consciously proud of his martyrdom. It soothed him paradoxically to tell himself that he was "cleaned"; that Marie had ruined him absolutely, and that he was just ten dollars and a decent suit or two of clothes better off than a tramp. He was tempted to go back and send the ten dollars after the rest of the fifteen hundred, but good sense prevailed. He would have to borrow money for his next meal, if he did that, and Bud was touchy about such things.

He kept the ten dollars therefore, and went down to the garage where he felt most at home, and stood there with his hands in his pockets and the corners of his mouth tipped downward—normally they had a way of tipping upward, as though he was secretly amused at something—and his eyes sullen, though they carried tiny lines at the corners to show how they used to twinkle. He took the ten-dollar bank note from his pocket, straightened out the wrinkles and looked at it disdainfully. As plainly as though he spoke, his face told what he was thinking about it: that this was what a woman had brought him to! He crumpled it up and made a gesture as though he would throw it into the street, and a man behind him laughed abruptly. Bud scowled and turned toward him a belligerent glance, and the man stopped laughing as suddenly as he had begun.

"If you've got money to throw to the birds, brother, I guess I won't make the proposition I was going to make. Thought I could talk business to you, maybe— but I guess I better tie a can to that idea."

Bud grunted and put the ten dollars in his pocket.

"What idea's that?"

"Oh, driving a car I'm taking south. Sprained my shoulder, and don't feel like tackling it myself. They tell me in here that you aren't doing anything now—" He made the pause that asks for an answer.

"They told you right. I've done it."

The man's eyebrows lifted, but since Bud did not explain, he went on with his own explanation.

"You don't remember me, but I rode into Big Basin with you last summer. I know you can drive, and it doesn't matter a lot whether it's asphalt or cow trail you drive over."

Bud was in too sour a mood to respond to the flattery. He did not even grunt.

"Could you take a car south for me? There'll be night driving, and bad roads, maybe—"

"If you know what you say you know about my driving, what's the idea—asking me if I can?"

"Well, put it another way. Will you?"

"You're on. Where's the car? Here?" Bud sent a seeking look into the depths of the garage. He knew every car in there. "What is there in it for me?" he added perfunctorily, because he would have gone just for sake of getting a free ride rather than stay in San Jose over night.

"There's good money in it, if you can drive with your mouth shut. This isn't any booster parade. Fact is—let's walk to the depot, while I tell you." He stepped out of the doorway, and Bud gloomily followed him. "Little trouble with my wife," the man explained apologetically. "Having me shadowed, and all that sort of thing. And I've got business south and want to be left alone to do it. Darn these women!" he exploded suddenly.

Bud mentally said amen, but kept his mouth shut upon his sympathy with the sentiment.

"Foster's my name. Now here's a key to the garage at this address." He handed Bud a padlock key and an address scribbled on a card. "That's my place in Oakland, out by Lake Merritt. You go there to-night, get the car, and have it down at the Broadway Wharf to meet the 11:30 boat—the one the theater crowd uses.

Have plenty of gas and oil; there won't be any stops after we start. Park out pretty well near the shore end as close as you can get to that ten-foot gum sign, and be ready to go when I climb in. I may have a friend with me. You know Oakland?"

"Fair to middling. I can get around by myself."

"Well, that's all right. I've got to go back to the city—catching the next train. You better take the two-fifty to Oakland. Here's money for whatever expense there is. And say! put these number plates in your pocket, and take off the ones on the car. I bought these of a fellow that had a smash—they'll do for the trip. Put them on, will you? She's wise to the car number, of course. Put the plates you take off under the seat cushion; don't leave 'em. Be just as careful as if it was a life-and-death matter, will you? I've got a big deal on, down there, and I don't want her spilling the beans just to satisfy a grudge—which she would do in a minute. So don't fail to be at the ferry, parked so you can slide out easy. Get down there by that big gum sign. I'll find you, all right."

"I'll be there." Bud thrust the key and another ten dollars into his pocket and turned away.

"And don't say anything—"

"Do I look like an open-faced guy?"

The man laughed. "Not much, or I wouldn't have picked you for the trip." He hurried down to the depot platform, for his train was already whistling, farther down the yards.

Bud looked after him, the corners of his mouth taking their normal, upward tilt. It began to look as though luck had not altogether deserted him, in spite of the recent blow it had given. He slid the wrapped number plates into the inside pocket of his overcoat, pushed his hands deep into his pockets, and walked up to the cheap hotel which had been his bleak substitute for a home during his trouble. He packed everything he owned—a big suitcase held it all by squeezing—paid his bill at the office, accepted a poor cigar, and in return said, yes, he was going to strike out and look for work; and took the train for Oakland.

A street car landed him within two blocks of the address on the tag, and Bud walked through thickening fog and dusk to the place. Foster had a good-looking house, he observed. Set back on the middle of two lots, it was, with a cement drive sloping up from the street to the garage backed against the alley. Under cover of lighting a cigarette, he inspected the place before he ventured farther. The blinds were drawn down—at least upon the side next the drive. On the other he thought he caught a gleam of light at the rear; rather, the beam that came from a gleam of light in Foster's dining room or kitchen shining on the next house. But he was not certain of it, and the absolute quiet reassured him so that he went up the drive, keeping on the grass border until he reached the garage. This, he told himself, was just like a woman—raising the deuce around so that a man had to sneak into his own place to get his own car out of his own garage. If Foster was up against the kind of deal Bud had been up against, he sure had Bud's sympathy, and he sure would get the best help Bud was capable of giving him.

The key fitted the lock, and Bud went in, set down his suitcase, and closed the door after him. It was dark as a pocket in there, save where a square of grayness betrayed a window. Bud felt his way to the side of the car, groped to the robe rail, found a heavy, fringed robe, and curtained the window until he could see no thread of light anywhere; after which he ventured to use his flashlight until he had found the switch and turned on the light.

There was a little side door at the back, and it was fastened on the inside with a stout hook. Bud thought for a minute, took a long chance, and let himself out into the yard, closing the door after him. He walked around the garage to the front and satisfied himself that the light inside did not show. Then he went around the back of the house and found that he had not been mistaken about the light. The house was certainly occupied, and like the neighboring houses seemed concerned only with the dinner hour of the inmates. He went back, hooked the little door on the inside, and began a careful inspection of the car he was to drive.

It was a big, late-modeled touring car, of the kind that sells for nearly five thousand dollars. Bud's eyes lightened with satisfaction when he looked at it. There would be pleasure as well as profit in driving this old girl to Los Angeles, he told himself. It fairly made his mouth water to look at her standing there. He got in and slid behind the wheel and fingered the gear lever, and tested the clutch and the foot brake—not because he doubted them, but because he had a hankering to feel their smoothness of operation. Bud loved a good car just as he had loved a good horse in the years behind him. Just as he used to walk around a good horse and pat its sleek shoulder and feel the hard muscles of its trim legs, so now he made love to this big car. Let that old hen of Foster's crab the trip south? He should sa-a-ay not!

There did not seem to be a thing that he could do to her, but nevertheless he got down and, gave all the grease cups a turn, removed the number plates and put them under the rear seat cushion, inspected the gas tank and the oil gauge and the fanbelt and the radiator, turned back the trip-mileage to zero—professional driving had made Bud careful as a taxi driver about recording the mileage of a trip—looked at the clock set in the instrument board, and pondered.

What if the old lady took a notion to drive somewhere? She would miss the car and raise a hullabaloo, and maybe crab the whole thing in the start. In that case, Bud decided that the best way would be to let her go. He could pile on to the empty trunk rack behind, and manage somehow to get off with the car when she stopped. Still, there was not much chance of her going out in the fog—and now that he listened, he heard the drip of rain. No, there was not much chance. Foster had not seemed to think there was any chance of the car being in use, and Foster ought to know. He would wait until about ten-thirty, to play safe, and then go.

Rain spelled skid chains to Bud. He looked in the tool box, found a set, and put them on. Then, because he was not going to take any chances, he put another set, that he found hanging up, on the front wheels. After that he turned out the light, took down the robe and wrapped himself in it, and laid himself down on the rear seat to wait for ten-thirty.

He dozed, and the next he knew there was a fumbling at the door in front, and the muttering of a voice. Bud slid noiselessly out of the car and under it, head to the rear where he could crawl out quickly. The voice sounded like a man, and presently the door opened and Bud was sure of it. He caught a querulous sentence or two.

"Door left unlocked—the ignorant hound—Good thing I don't trust him too far—" Some one came fumbling in and switched on the light. "Careless hound—told him to be careful—never even put the robe on the rail where it belongs—and then they howl about the way they're treated! Want more wages—don't earn what they do get—"

Bud, twisting his head, saw a pair of slippered feet beside the running board. The owner of the slippers was folding the robe and laying it over the rail, and grumbling to himself all the while. "Have to come out in the rain—daren't trust him an inch—just like him to go off and leave the door unlocked—" With a last grunt or two the mumbling ceased. The light was switched off, and Bud heard the doors pulled shut, and the rattle of the padlock and chain. He waited another minute and crawled out.

"Might have told me there was a father-in-law in the outfit," he grumbled to himself. "Big a butt-in as Marie's mother, at that. Huh. Never saw my suit case, never noticed the different numbers, never got next to the chains—huh! Regular old he-hen, and I sure don't blame Foster for wanting to tie a can to the bunch."

Very cautiously he turned his flashlight on the face of the automobile clock. The hour hand stood a little past ten, and Bud decided he had better go. He would have to fill the gas tank, and get more oil, and he wanted to test the air in his tires. No stops after they started, said Foster; Bud had set his heart on showing Foster something in the way of getting a car over the road.

Father-in-law would holler if he heard the car, but Bud did not intend that father-in-law should hear it. He would much rather run the gauntlet of that driveway then wait in the dark any longer. He remembered the slope down to the street, and grinned contentedly. He would give father-in-law a chance to throw a fit, next morning.

He set his suit case in the tonneau, went out of the little door, edged around to the front and very, very cautiously he unlocked the big doors and set them open. He went in and felt the front wheels, judged that they were set straight, felt around the interior until his fingers touched a block of wood and stepped off the approximate length of the car in front of the garage, allowing for the swing of the doors, and placed the block there. Then he went back, eased off the emergency brake, grabbed a good handhold and strained forward.

The chains hindered, but the floor sloped to the front a trifle, which helped. In a moment he had the satisfaction of feeling the big car give, then roll slowly ahead. The front wheels dipped down over the threshold, and Bud stepped upon the running board, took the wheel, and by instinct more than by sight guided her through the doorway without a scratch. She rolled forward like a black shadow until a wheel jarred against the block, whereupon he set the emergency brake and got off, breathing free once more. He picked up the block and carried it back, quietly closed the big doors and locked them, taking time to do it silently. Then, in a glow of satisfaction with his work, he climbed slowly into the car, settled down luxuriously in the driver's seat, eased off the brake, and with a little lurch of his body forward started the car rolling down the driveway.

There was a risk, of course, in coasting out on to the street with no lights, but he took it cheerfully, planning to dodge if he saw the lights of another car coming. It pleased him to remember that the street inclined toward the bay. He rolled past the house without a betraying sound, dipped over the curb to the asphalt, swung the car townward, and coasted nearly half a block with the ignition switch on before he pushed up the throttle, let in his clutch, and got the answering chug-chug of the engine. With the lights on full he went purring down the street in the misty fog, pleased with himself and his mission.

CHAPTER FOUR.

HEAD SOUTH AND KEEP GOING

At a lunch wagon down near the water front, Bud stopped and bought two "hot dog" sandwiches and a mug of hot coffee boiled with milk in it and sweetened with three cubes of sugar. "O-oh, boy!" he ejaculated gleefully when he set his teeth into biscuit and hot hamburger. Leaning back luxuriously in the big car, he ate and drank until he could eat and drink no more. Then, with a bag of bananas on the seat beside him, he drove on down to the mole, searching through the drizzle for the big gum sign which Foster had named. Just even with the coughing engine of a waiting through train he saw it, and backed in against the curb, pointing the car's radiator toward the mainland. He had still half an hour to wait, and he buttoned on the curtains of the car, since a wind from across the bay was sending the drizzle slantwise; moreover it occurred to him that Foster would not object to the concealment while they were passing through Oakland. Then he listlessly ate a banana while he waited.

The hoarse siren of a ferryboat bellowed through the murk. Bud started the engine, throttled it down to his liking, and left it to warm up for the flight. He ate another banana, thinking lazily that he wished he owned this car. For the first time in many a day his mind was not filled and boiling over with his trouble. Marie and all the bitterness she had come to mean to him receded into the misty background of his mind and hovered there, an indistinct memory of something painful in his life.

A street car slipped past, bobbing down the track like a duck sailing over ripples. A local train clanged down to the depot and stood jangling its bell while it disgorged passengers for the last boat to the City whose wall of stars was hidden behind the drizzle and the clinging fog. People came straggling down the sidewalk—not many, for few had business with the front end of the waiting trains. Bud pushed the throttle up a little. His fingers dropped down to the gear lever, his foot snuggled against the clutch pedal.

Feet came hurrying. Two voices mumbled together. "Here he is," said one. "That's the number I gave him." Bud felt some one step hurriedly upon the running board. The tonneau door was yanked open. A man puffed audibly behind him. "Yuh ready?" Foster's voice hissed in Bud's ear.

"R'aring to go." Bud heard the second man get in and shut the door, and he jerked the gear lever into low. His foot came gently back with the clutch, and the car slid out and away.

Foster settled back on the cushions with a sigh. The other man was fumbling the side curtains, swearing under his breath when his fingers bungled the fastenings.

"Everything all ready?" Foster's voice was strident with anxiety.

"Sure thing."

"Well, head south—any road you know best. And keep going, till I tell you to stop. How's the oil and gas?"

"Full up. Gas enough for three hundred miles. Extra gallon of oil in the car. What d'yah want—the speed limit through town?"

"Nah. Side streets, if you know any. They might get quick action and telephone ahead."

"Leave it to me, brother."

Bud did not know for sure, never having been pursued; but it seemed to him that a straightaway course down a main street where other cars were scudding homeward would be the safest route, because the simplest. He did not want any side streets in his, he decided—and maybe run into a mess of street-improvement litter, and have to back trail around it. He held the car to a hurry-home pace that was well within the law, and worked into the direct route to Hayward. He sensed that either Foster or his friend turned frequently to look back through the square celluloid window, but he did not pay much attention to them, for the streets were greasy with wet, and not all drivers would equip with four skid chains. Keeping sharp lookout for skidding cars and unexpected pedestrians and street-car crossings and the like fully occupied Bud.

For all that, an occasional mutter came unheeded to his ears, the closed curtains preserving articulate sounds like room walls.

"He's all right," he heard Foster whisper once. "Better than if he was in on it." He did not know that Foster was speaking of him.

"—if he gets next," the friend mumbled.

"Ah, quit your worrying," Foster grunted. "The trick's turned; that's something."

Bud was under the impression that they were talking about father-in-law, who had called Foster a careless hound; but whether they were or not concerned him so little that his own thoughts never flagged in their shuttle-weaving through his mind. The mechanics of handling the big car and getting the best speed out of her with the least effort and risk, the tearing away of the last link of his past happiness and his grief; the feeling that this night was the real parting between him and Marie, the real stepping out into the future; the future itself, blank beyond the end of this trip, these were quite enough to hold Bud oblivious to the conversation of strangers.

At dawn they neared a little village. Through this particular county the road was unpaved and muddy, and the car was a sight to behold. The only clean spot was on the windshield, where Bud had reached around once or twice with a handful of waste and cleaned a place to see through. It was raining soddenly, steadily, as though it always had rained and always would rain.

Bud turned his face slightly to one side. "How about stopping; I'll have to feed her some oil—and it wouldn't hurt to fill the gas tank again. These heavy roads eat up a lot of extra power. What's her average mileage on a gallon, Foster?"

"How the deuce should I know?" Foster snapped, just coming out of a doze.

"You ought to know, with your own car—and gas costing what it does."

"Oh!—ah—what was it you asked?" Foster yawned aloud. "I musta been asleep."

"I guess you musta been, all right," Bud grunted. "Do you want breakfast here, or don't you? I've got to stop for gas and oil; that's what I was asking?"

The two consulted together, and finally told Bud to stop at the first garage and get his oil and gas. After that he could drive to a drug store and buy a couple of thermos bottles, and after that he could go to the nearest restaurant and get the bottles filled with black coffee, and have lunch put up for six people. Foster and his friend would remain in the car.

Bud did these things, revising the plan to the extent of eating his own breakfast at the counter in the restaurant while the lunch was being prepared in the kitchen.

From where he sat he could look across at the muddy car standing before a closed millinery-and-drygoods store. It surely did not look much like the immaculate machine he had gloated over the evening before, but it was a powerful, big brute of a car and looked its class in every line. Bud was proud to drive a car like that. The curtains were buttoned down tight, and he thought amusedly of the two men huddled inside, shivering and hungry, yet refusing to come in and get warmed up with a decent breakfast. Foster, he thought, must certainly be scared of his wife, if he daren't show himself in this little rube town. For the first time Bud had a vagrant suspicion that Foster had not told quite all there was to tell about this trip. Bud wondered now if Foster was not going to meet a "Jane" somewhere in the South. That terrifying Mann Act would account for his caution much better than would the business deal of which Foster had hinted.

Of course, Bud told himself while the waiter refilled his coffee cup, it was none of his business what Foster had up his sleeve. He wanted to get somewhere quickly and quietly, and Bud was getting him there. That was all he need to consider. Warmed and once more filled with a sense of well-being, Bud made himself a cigarette before the lunch was ready, and with his arms full of food he went out and across the street. Just before he reached the car one of the thermos bottles started to slide down under his elbow. Bud attempted to grip it against his ribs, but the thing had developed a slipperiness that threatened the whole load, so he stopped to rearrange his packages, and got an irritated sentence or two from his passengers.

"Giving yourself away like that! Why couldn't you fake up a mileage? Everybody lies or guesses about the gas—"

"Aw, what's the difference? The simp ain't next to anything. He thinks I own it."

"Well, don't make the mistake of thinking he's a sheep. Once he—"

Bud suddenly remembered that he wanted something more from the restaurant, and returned forth-with, slipping thermos bottle and all. He bought two packages of chewing gum to while away the time when he could not handily smoke, and when he returned to the car he went muttering disapproving remarks about the rain and the mud and the bottles. He poked his head under the front curtain and into a glum silence. The two men leaned back into the two corners of the wide seat, with their heads drawn down into their coat collars and their hands thrust under the robe. Foster reached forward and took a thermos bottle, his partner seized another.

"Say, you might get us a bottle of good whisky, too," said Foster, holding out a small gold piece between his gloved thumb and finger. "Be quick about it though—we want to be traveling. Lord, it's cold!"

Bud went into a saloon a few doors up the street, and was back presently with the bottle and the change. There being nothing more to detain them there, he kicked some of the mud off his feet, scraped off the rest on the edge of the running board and climbed in, fastening the curtain against the storm. "Lovely weather," he grunted sarcastically. "Straight on to Bakersfield, huh?"

There was a minute of silence save for the gurgling of liquid running out of a bottle into an eager mouth. Bud laid an arm along the back of his seat and waited, his head turned toward them. "Where are you fellows going, anyway?" he asked impatiently.

"Los An—" the stranger gurgled, still drinking.

"Yuma!" snapped Foster. "You shut up, Mert. I'm running this."

"Better—"

"Yuma. You hit the shortest trail for Yuma, Bud. I'm running this."

Foster seemed distinctly out of humor. He told Mert again to shut up, and Mert did so grumblingly, but somewhat diverted and consoled, Bud fancied, by the sandwiches and coffee—and the whisky too, he guessed. For presently there was an odor from the uncorked bottle in the car.

Bud started and drove steadily on through the rain that never ceased. The big car warmed his heart with its perfect performance, its smooth, effortless speed, its ease of handling. He had driven too long and too constantly to tire easily, and he was almost tempted to settle down to sheer enjoyment in driving such a car. Last night he had enjoyed it, but last night was not to-day.

He wished he had not overheard so much, or else had overheard more. He was inclined to regret his retreat from the acrimonious voices as being premature. Just why was he a simp, for instance? Was it because he thought Foster owned the car? Bud wondered whether father-in-law had not bought it, after all. Now that he began thinking from a different angle, he remembered that father-in-law had behaved very much like the proud possessor of a new car. It really did not look plausible that he would come out in the drizzle to see if Foster's car was safely locked in for the night. There had been, too, a fussy fastidiousness in the way the robe had been folded and hung over the rail. No man would do that for some other man's property, unless he was paid for it.

Wherefore, Bud finally concluded that Foster was not above helping himself to family property. On the whole, Bud did not greatly disapprove of that; he was too actively resentful of his own mother-in-law. He was not sure but he might have done something of the sort himself, if his mother-in-law had possessed a six-thousand-dollar car. Still, such a car generally means a good deal to the owner, and he did not wonder that Foster was nervous about it.

But in the back of his mind there lurked a faint dissatisfaction with this easy explanation. It occurred to him that if there was going to be any trouble about the car, he might be involved beyond the point of comfort. After all, he did not know Foster, and he had no more reason for believing Foster's story than he had for doubting. For all he knew, it might not be a wife that Foster was so afraid of.

Bud was not stupid. He was merely concerned chiefly with his own affairs—a common enough failing, surely. But now that he had thought himself into a mental eddy where his own affairs offered no new impulse toward emotion, he turned over and over in his mind the mysterious trip he was taking. It had come to seem just a little too mysterious to suit him; and when Bud Moore was not suited he was apt to do something about it.

What he did in this case was to stop in Bakersfield at a garage that had a combination drugstore and news-stand next door. He explained shortly to his companions that he had to stop and buy a road map and that he wouldn't be long, and crawled out into the rain. At the open doorway of the garage he turned and looked at the car. No, it certainly did not look in the least like the machine he had driven down to the Oakland mole—except, of course, that it was big and of the same make. It might have been empty, too, for all the sign it gave of being occupied. Foster and Mert evidently had no intention whatever of showing themselves.

Bud went into the drugstore, remained there for five minutes perhaps, and emerged with a morning paper which he rolled up and put into his pocket. He had glanced through its feature news, and had read hastily one front-page article that had nothing whatever to do with the war, but told about the daring robbery of a jewelry store in San Francisco the night before.

The safe, it seemed, had been opened almost in plain sight of the street crowds, with the lights full on in the store. A clever arrangement of two movable mirrors had served to shield the thief—or thieves. For no longer than two or three minutes, it seemed, the lights had been off, and it was thought that the raiders had used the interval of darkness to move the mirrors into position. Which went far toward proving that the crime had been carefully planned in advance. Furthermore, the article stated with some assurance that trusted employees were involved.

Bud also had glanced at the news items of less importance, and had been startled enough—yet not so much surprised as he would have been a few hours earlier—to read, under the caption: DARING THIEF STEALS COSTLY CAR, to learn that a certain rich man of Oakland had lost his new automobile. The address of the bereaved man had been given, and Bud's heart had given a flop when he read it. The details of the theft had not been told, but Bud never noticed their absence. His memory supplied all that for him with sufficient vividness.

He rolled a cigarette, lighted it, and with the paper stuffed carelessly into his pocket he went to the car, climbed in, and drove on to the south, just as matter-of-factly as though he had not just then discovered that he, Bud Moore, had stolen a six-thousand-dollar automobile the night before.

CHAPTER FIVE.
BUD CANNOT PERFORM MIRACLES

They went on and on, through the rain and the wind, sometimes through the mud as well, where the roads were not paved. Foster had almost pounced upon the newspaper when he discovered it in Bud's pocket as he climbed in, and Bud knew that the two read that feature article avidly. But if they had any comments to make, they saved them for future privacy. Beyond a few muttered sentences they were silent.

Bud did not care whether they talked or not. They might have talked themselves hoarse, when it came to that, without changing his opinions or his attitude toward them. He had started out the most unsuspecting of men, and now he was making up for it by suspecting Foster and Mert of being robbers and hypocrites and potential murderers. He could readily imagine them shooting him in the back of the head while he drove, if that would suit their purpose, or if they thought that he suspected them.

He kept reviewing his performance in that garage. Had he really intended to steal the car, he would not have had the nerve to take the chances he had taken. He shivered when he recalled how he had slid under the car when the owner came in. What if the man had seen him or heard him? He would be in jail now, instead of splashing along the highway many miles to the south. For that matter, he was likely to land in jail, anyway, before he was done with Foster, unless he did some pretty close figuring. Wherefore he drove with one part of his brain, and with the other he figured upon how he was going to get out of the mess himself—and land Foster and Mert deep in the middle of it. For such was his vengeful desire.

After an hour or so, when his stomach began to hint that it was eating time for healthy men, he slowed down and turned his head toward the tonneau. There they were, hunched down under the robe, their heads drawn into their collars like two turtles half asleep on a mud bank.

"Say, how about some lunch?" he demanded. "Maybe you fellows can get along on whisky and sandwiches, but I'm doing the work; and if you notice, I've been doing it for about twelve hours now without any let-up. There's a town ahead here a ways—"

"Drive around it, then," growled Foster, lifting his chin to stare ahead through the fogged windshield. "We've got hot coffee here, and there's plenty to eat. Enough for two meals. How far have we come since we started?"

"Far enough to be called crazy if we go much farther without a square meal," Bud snapped. Then he glanced at the rumpled newspaper and added carelessly, "Anything new in the paper?"

"No!" Mert spoke up sharply. "Go on. You're doing all right so far—don't spoil it by laying down on your job!"

"Sure, go on!" Foster urged. "We'll stop when we get away from this darn burg, and you can rest your legs a little while we eat."

Bud went on, straight through the middle of the town without stopping. They scurried down a long, dismal lane toward a low-lying range of hills pertly wooded with bald patches of barren earth and rock. Beyond were mountains which Bud guessed was the Tehachapi range. Beyond them, he believed he would find desert and desertion. He had never been over this road before, so he could no more than guess. He knew that the ridge road led to Los Angeles, and he did not want anything of that road. Too many travelers. He swung into a decent-looking road that branched off to the left, wondering where it led, but not greatly caring. He kept that road until they had climbed over a ridge or two and were in the mountains. Soaked wilderness lay all about them, green in places where grass would grow, brushy in places, barren and scarred with outcropping ledges, pencilled with wire fences drawn up over high knolls.

In a sequestered spot where the road hugged close the concave outline of a bushy bluff, Bud slowed and turned out behind a fringe of bushes, and stopped.

"This is safe enough," he announced, "and my muscles are kinda crampy. I'll tell the world that's been quite some spell of straight driving."

Mert grunted, but Foster was inclined to cheerfulness. "You're some driver, Bud. I've got to hand it to you."

Bud grinned. "All right, I'll take it—half of it, anyway, if you don't mind. You must remember I don't know you fellows. Most generally I collect half in advance, on a long trip like this." Foster's eyes opened, but he reached obediently inside his coat. Mert growled inaudible comments upon Bud's nerve.

"Oh, we can't kick, Mert," Foster smoothed him down diplomatically. "He's delivered the goods, so far. And he certainly does know how to put a car over the road. He don't know us, remember!"

Mert grunted again and subsided. Foster extracted a bank note from his bill-folder, which Bud observed had a prosperous plumpness, and held it out to Bud.

"I guess fifty dollars won't hurt your feelings, will it, brother? That's more than you'd charge for twice the trip, but we appreciate a tight mouth, and the hurry-up trip you've made of it, and all that It's special work, and we're willing to pay a special price. See?"

"Sure. But I only want half, right now. Maybe," he added with the lurking twinkle in his eyes, "I won't suit yuh quite so well the rest of the way. I'll have to go b'-guess and b'-gosh from here on. I've got some change left from what I bought for yuh this morning too. Wait till I check up."

Very precisely he did so, and accepted enough from Foster to make up the amount to twenty-five dollars. He was tempted to take more. For one minute he even contemplated holding the two up and taking enough to salve his hurt pride and his endangered reputation. But he did not do anything of the sort, of course; let's believe he was too honest to do it even in revenge for the scurvy trick they had played him.

He ate a generous lunch of sandwiches and dill pickles and a wedge of taste-less cocoanut cake, and drank half a pint or so of the hot, black coffee, and felt more cheerful.

"Want to get down and stretch your legs? I've got to take a look at the tires, anyway. Thought she was riding like one was kinda flat, the last few miles."

They climbed out stiffly into the rain, stood around the car and stared at it and at Bud testing his tires, and walked off down the road for a little distance where they stood talking earnestly together. From the corner of his eye Bud caught Mert tilting his head that way, and smiled to himself. Of course they were talking about him! Any fool would know that much. Also they were discussing the best means of getting rid of him, or of saddling upon him the crime of stealing the car, or some other angle at which he touched their problem.

Under cover of testing the rear wheel farthest from them, he peeked into the tonneau and took a good look at the small traveling bag they had kept on the seat between them all the way. He wished he dared—But they were coming back, as if they would not trust him too long alone with that bag. He bent again to the tire, and when they climbed back into the curtained car he was getting the pump tubing out to pump up that particular tire a few pounds.

They did not pay much attention to him. They seemed preoccupied and not too friendly with each other, Bud thought. Their general air of gloom he could of course lay to the weather and the fact that they had been traveling for about fourteen hours without any rest; but there was something more than that in the atmosphere. He thought they had disagreed, and that he was the subject of their disagreement.

He screwed down the valve cap, coiled the pump tube and stowed it away in the tool box, opened the gas tank, and looked in—and right there he did some-thing else; something that would have spelled disaster if either of them had seen him do it. He spilled a handful of little round white objects like marbles into the tank before he screwed on the cap, and from his pocket he pulled a little paper box, crushed it in his hand, and threw it as far as he could into the bushes. Then, whistling just above his breath, which was a habit with Bud when his work was going along pleasantly, he scraped the mud off his feet, climbed in, and drove on down the road.

The big car picked up speed on the down grade, racing along as though the short rest had given it a fresh enthusiasm for the long road that wound in and out and up and down and seemed to have no end. As though he joyed in putting her over the miles, Bud drove. Came a hill, he sent her up it with a devil-may-care confidence, swinging around curves with a squall of the powerful horn that made cattle feeding half a mile away on the slopes lift their startled heads and look.

"How much longer are you good for, Bud?" Foster leaned forward to ask, his tone flattering with the praise that was in it.

"Me? As long as this old boat will travel," Bud flung back gleefully, giving her a little more speed as they rocked over a culvert and sped away to the next hill. He chuckled, but Foster had settled back again satisfied, and did not notice.

Halfway up the next hill the car slowed suddenly, gave a snort, gasped twice as Bud retarded the spark to help her out, and, died. She was a heavy car to hold on that stiff grade, and in spite of the full emergency brake helped out with the service brake, she inched backward until the rear wheels came full against a hump across the road and held.

Bud did not say anything; your efficient chauffeur reserves his eloquence for something more complex than a dead engine. He took down the curtain on that side, leaned out into the rain and inspected the road behind him, shifted into reverse, and backed to the bottom.

"What's wrong?" Foster leaned forward to ask senselessly.

"When I hit level ground, I'm going to find out," Bud retorted, still watching the road and steering with one hand. "Does the old girl ever cut up with you on hills?"

"Why—no. She never has," Foster answered dubiously.

"Reason I asked, she didn't just choke down from the pull. She went and died on me."

"That's funny," Foster observed weakly.

On the level Bud went into neutral and pressed the self-starter with a pessimistic deliberation. He got three chugs and a backfire into the carburetor, and after that silence. He tried it again, coaxing her with the spark and throttle. The engine gave a snort, hesitated and then, quite suddenly, began to throb with docile regularity that seemed to belie any previous intention of "cutting up."

Bud fed her the gas and took a run at the hill. She went up like a thoroughbred and died at the top, just when the road had dipped into the descent. Bud sent her down hill on compression, but at the bottom she refused to find her voice again when he turned on the switch and pressed the accelerator. She simply rolled down to the first incline and stopped there like a balky mule.

"Thunder!" said Bud, and looked around at Foster. "Do you reckon the old boat is jinxed, just because I said I could drive her as far as she'd go? The old rip ain't shot a cylinder since we hit the top of the hill."

"Maybe the mixture—"

"Yeah," Bud interrupted with a secret grin, "I've been wondering about that, and the needle valve, and the feed pipe, and a few other little things. Well, we'll have a look."

Forthwith he climbed out into the drizzle and began a conscientious search for the trouble. He inspected the needle valve with much care, and had Foster on the front seat trying to start her afterwards. He looked for short circuit. He changed the carburetor adjustment, and Foster got a weary chug-chug that ceased almost as soon as it had begun. He looked all the spark plugs over, he went after the vacuum feed and found that working perfectly. He stood back, finally, with his hands on his hips, and stared at the engine and shook his head slowly twice.

Foster, in the driver's seat, swore and tried again to start it. "Maybe if you cranked it," he suggested tentatively.

"What for? The starter turns her over all right. Spark's all right too, strong and hot. However—" With a sigh of resignation Bud got out what tools he wanted and went to work. Foster got out and stood around, offering suggestions that were too obvious to be of much use, but which Bud made it a point to follow as far as was practicable.

Foster said it must be the carburetor, and Bud went relentlessly after the carburetor. He impressed Foster with the fact that he knew cars, and when he told Foster to get in and try her again, Foster did so with the air of having seen the end of the trouble. At first it did seem so, for the engine started at once and worked smoothly until Bud had gathered his wrenches off the running board and was climbing it, when it slowed down and stopped, in spite of Foster's frantic efforts to keep it alive with spark and throttle.

"Good Glory!" cried Bud, looking reproachfully in at Foster. "What'd yuh want to stop her for?"

"I didn't!" Foster's consternation was ample proof of his innocence. "What the devil ails the thing?"

"You tell me, and I'll fix it," Bud retorted savagely. Then he smoothed his manner and went back to the carburetor. "Acts like the gas kept choking off," he said, "but it ain't that. She's O.K. I know, 'cause I've tested it clean back to tank. There's nothing the matter with the feed—she's getting gas same as she has all along. I can take off the mag. and see if anything's wrong there; but I'm pretty sure there ain't. Couldn't any water or mud get in—not with that oil pan perfect. She looks dry as a bone, and clean. Try her again, Foster; wait till I set the spark about right. Now, you leave it there, and give her the gas kinda gradual, and catch her when she talks. We'll see—"

They saw that she was not going to "talk" at all. Bud swore a little and got out more tools and went after the magneto with grim determination. Again Foster climbed out and stood in the drizzle and watched him. Mert crawled over into the front seat where he could view the proceedings through the windshield. Bud glanced up and saw him there, and grinned maliciously. "Your friend seems to love wet weather same as a cat does," he observed to Foster. "He'll be terrible happy if you're stalled here till you get a tow in somewhere."

"It's your business to see that we aren't stalled," Mert snapped at him viciously. "You've got to make the thing go. You've got to!"

"Well, I ain't the Almighty," Bud retorted acidly. "I can't perform miracles while yuh wait."

"Starting a cranky car doesn't take a miracle," whined Mert. "Anybody that knows cars—"

"She's no business to be a cranky car," Foster interposed pacifically. "Why, she's practically new!" He stepped over a puddle and stood beside Bud, peering down at the silent engine. "Have you looked at the intake valve?" he asked pathetically.

"Why, sure. It's all right. Everything's all right, as far as I can find out." Bud looked Foster straight in the eye—and if his own were a bit anxious, that was to be expected.

"Everything's all right," he added measuredly. "Only, she won't go." He waited, watching Foster's face.

Foster chewed a corner of his lip worriedly. "Well, what do you make of it?" His tone was helpless.

Bud threw out his two hands expressively, and shook his head. He let down the hood, climbed in, slid into the driver's seat, and went through the operation of starting. Only, he didn't start. The self-starter hummed as it spun the flywheel, but nothing whatever was elicited save a profane phrase from Foster and a growl from Mert. Bud sat back flaccid, his whole body owning defeat.

"Well, that means a tow in to the nearest shop," he stated, after a minute of dismal silence. "She's dead as a doornail."

Mert sat back in his corner of the seat, muttering into his collar. Foster looked at him, looked at Bud, looked at the car and at the surrounding hills. He seemed terribly depressed and at the same time determined to make the best of things. Bud could almost pity him—almost.

"Do you know how far it is back to that town we passed?" he asked Bud spiritlessly after a while. Bud looked at the speedometer, made a mental calculation and told him it was fifteen miles. Towns, it seemed, were rather far apart in this section of the country.

"Well, let's see the road map. How far is it to the next one?"

"Search me. They didn't have any road maps back there. Darned hick burg."

Foster studied awhile. "Well, let's see if we can push her off the middle of the road—and then I guess we'll have to let you walk back and get help. Eh, Mert? There's nothing else we can do—"

"What yuh going to tell 'em?" Mert demanded suspiciously.

Bud permitted a surprised glance to slant back at Mert. "Why, whatever you fellows fake up for me to tell," he said naively. "I know the truth ain't popular on this trip, so get together and dope out something. And hand me over my suit case, will yuh? I want some dry socks to put on when I get there."

Foster very obligingly tilted the suit case over into the front seat. After that he and Mert, as by a common thought impelled, climbed out and went over to a bushy live oak to confer in privacy. Mert carried the leather bag with him.

By the time they had finished and were coming back, Bud had gone through his belongings and had taken out a few letters that might prove awkward if found there later, two pairs of socks and his razor and toothbrush. He was folding the socks to stow away in his pocket when they got in.

"You can say that we're from Los Angeles, and on our way home," Foster told him curtly. It was evident to Bud that the two had not quite agreed upon some subject they had discussed. "That's all right. I'm Foster, and he's named Brown—if any one gets too curious."

"Fine. Fine because it's so simple. I'll eat another sandwich, if you don't mind, before I go. I'll tell a heartless world that fifteen miles is some little stroll—for a guy that hates walkin'."

"You're paid for it," Mert growled at him rudely.

"Sure, I'm paid for it," Bud assented placidly, taking a bite. They might have wondered at his calm, but they did not. He ate what he wanted, took a long drink of the coffee, and started off up the hill they had rolled down an hour or more past.

He walked briskly, and when he was well out of earshot Bud began to whistle. Now and then he stopped to chuckle, and sometimes he frowned at an uncomfortable thought. But on the whole he was very well pleased with his present circumstances.

CHAPTER SIX.

BUD TAKES TO THE HILLS

In a little village which he had glimpsed from the top of a hill Bud went into the cluttered little general store and bought a few blocks of slim, evil smelling matches and a couple of pounds of sliced bacon, a loaf of stale bread, and two small cans of baked beans. He stuffed them all into the pocket of his overcoat, and went out and hunted up a long-distance telephone sign. It had not taken him more than an hour to walk to the town, for he had only to follow a country road that branched off that way for a couple of miles down a valley. There was a post office and the general store and a couple of saloons and a blacksmith shop that was thinking of turning into a garage but had gone no further than to hang out a sign that gasoline was for sale there. It was all very sordid and very lifeless and altogether discouraging in the drizzle of late afternoon. Bud did not see half a dozen human beings on his way to the telephone office, which he found was in the post office.

He called up San Francisco, and got the chief of police's office on the wire, and told them where they would find the men who had robbed that jewelry store of all its diamonds and some other unset jewels. Also he mentioned the car that was stolen, and that was now stalled and waiting for some kind soul to come and give it a tow.

He speedily had all the attention of the chief, and having thought out in advance his answers to certain pertinent questions, he did not stutter when they were asked. Yes, he had been hired to drive the ear south, and he had overheard enough to make him suspicious on the way. He knew that they had stolen the car. He was not absolutely sure that they were the diamond thieves but it would be easy enough to find out, because officers sent after them would naturally be mistaken for first aid from some garage, and the cops could nab the men and look into that grip they were so careful not to let out of their sight.

"Are you sure they won't get the car repaired and go on?" It was perfectly natural that the chief should fear that very thing.

"No chance!" Bud chuckled into the 'phone. "Not a chance in the world, chief. They'll be right there where I left 'em, unless some car comes along and gives 'em a tow. And if that happens you'll be able to trace 'em." He started to hang up, and added another bit of advice. "Say, chief, you better tell whoever gets the car, to empty the gas tank and clean out the carburetor and vacuum feed—and she'll go, all right! Adios."

He hung up and paid the charge hurriedly, and went out and down a crooked little lane that led between bushes to a creek and heavy timber. It did not seem to him advisable to linger; the San Francisco chief of police might set some officer in that village on his trail, just as a matter of precaution. Bud told himself that he would do it were he in the chief's place. When he reached the woods along the creek he ran, keeping as much as possible on thick leaf mold that left the least impression. He headed to the east, as nearly as he could judge, and when he came to a rocky canyon he struck into it.

He presently found himself in a network of small gorges that twisted away into the hills without any system whatever, as far as he could see. He took one that seemed to lead straightest toward where the sun would rise next morning, and climbed laboriously deeper and deeper into the hills. After awhile he had to descend from the ridge where he found himself standing bleakly revealed against a lowering, slaty sky that dripped rain incessantly. As far as he could see were hills and more hills, bald and barren except in certain canyons whose deeper shadows told of timber. Away off to the southwest a bright light showed briefly—the headlight of a Santa Fe train, he guessed it must be. To the east, which he faced, the land was broken with bare hills that fell just short of being mountains. He went down the first canyon that opened in that direction, ploughing doggedly ahead into the unknown.

That night Bud camped in the lee of a bank that was fairly well screened with rocks and bushes, and dined off broiled bacon and bread and a can of beans with tomato sauce, and called it a meal. At first he was not much inclined to take the risk of having a fire big enough to keep him warm. Later in the night he was perfectly willing to take the risk, but could not find enough dry wood. His rainproofed overcoat became quite soggy and damp on the inside, in spite of his efforts to shield himself from the rain. It was not exactly a comfortable night, but he worried through it somehow.

At daylight he opened another can of beans and made himself two thick bean sandwiches, and walked on while he ate them slowly. They tasted mighty good, Bud thought—but he wished fleetingly that he was back in the little green cottage on North Sixth Street, getting his own breakfast. He felt as though he could drink about four cups of coffee; and as to hotcakes—! But breakfast in the little green cottage recalled Marie, and Marie was a bitter memory. All the more bitter because he did not know where burrowed the root of his hot resentment. In a strong man's love for his home and his mate was it rooted, and drew therefrom the wormwood of love thwarted and spurned.

After awhile the high air currents flung aside the clouds like curtains before a doorway. The sunlight flashed out dazzlingly and showed Bud that the world, even this tumbled world, was good to look upon. His instincts were all for the great outdoors, and from such the sun brings quick response. Bud lifted his head, looked out over the hills to where a bare plain stretched in the far distance, and went on more briskly.

He did not meet any one at all; but that was chiefly because he did not want to meet any one. He went with his ears and his eyes alert, and was not above hiding behind a clump of stunted bushes when two horsemen rode down a canyon trail just below him. Also he searched for roads and then avoided them. It would be a fat morsel for Marie and her mother to roll under their tongues, he told himself savagely, if he were arrested and appeared in the papers as one of that bunch of crooks!

Late that afternoon, by traveling steadily in one direction, he topped a low ridge and saw an arm of the desert thrust out to meet him. A scooped gully with gravelly sides and rocky bottom led down that way, and because his feet were sore from so much sidehill travel, Bud went down. He was pretty well fagged too, and ready to risk meeting men, if thereby he might gain a square meal. Though he was not starving, or anywhere near it, he craved warm food and hot coffee.

So when he presently came upon two sway-backed burros that showed the sweaty imprint of packsaddles freshly removed, and a couple of horses also sweat roughened, he straightway assumed that some one was making camp not far away. One of the horses was hobbled, and they were all eating hungrily the grass that grew along the gully's sides. Camp was not only close, but had not yet reached suppertime, Bud guessed from the well-known range signs.

Two or three minutes proved him right. He came upon a man just driving the last tent peg. He straightened up and stared at Bud unblinkingly for a few seconds.

"Howdy, howdy," he greeted him then with tentative friendliness, and went on with his work. "You lost?" he added carefully. A man walking down out of the barren hills, and carrying absolutely nothing in the way of camp outfit, was enough to whet the curiosity of any one who knew that country. At the same time curiosity that became too apparent might be extremely unwelcome. So many things may drive a man into the hills—but few of them would bear discussion with strangers.

"Yes. I am, and I ain't." Bud came up and stood with his hands in his coat pockets, and watched the old fellow start his fire.

"Yeah—how about some supper? If you am, and you ain't as hungry as you look—"

"I'll tell the world I am, and then some. I ain't had a square meal since yesterday morning, and I grabbed that at a quick-lunch joint. I'm open to supper engagements, brother."

"All right. There's a side of bacon in that kyack over there. Get it out and slice some off, and we'll have supper before you know it. We will," he added pessimistically, "if this dang brush will burn."

Bud found the bacon and cut according to his appetite. His host got out a blackened coffeepot and half filled it with water from a dented bucket, and balanced it on one side of the struggling fire. He remarked that they had had some rain, to which Bud agreed. He added gravely that he believed it was going to clear up, though—unless the wind swung back into the storm quarter. Bud again professed cheerfully to be in perfect accord. After which conversational sparring they fell back upon the little commonplaces of the moment.

Bud went into a brush patch and managed to glean an armful of nearly dry wood, which he broke up with the axe and fed to the fire, coaxing it into freer blazing. The stranger watched him unobtrusively, critically, pottering about while Bud fried the bacon.

"I guess you've handled a frying pan before, all right," he remarked at last, when the bacon was fried without burning.

Bud grinned. "I saw one in a store window once as I was going by," he parried facetiously. "That was quite a while back."

"Yeah. Well, how's your luck with bannock? I've got it all mixed."

"Dump her in here, ole-timer," cried Bud, holding out the frying pan emptied of all but grease. "Wish I had another hot skillet to turn over the top."

"I guess you've been there, all right," the other chuckled. "Well, I don't carry but the one frying pan. I'm equipped light, because I've got to outfit with grub, further along."

"Well, we'll make out all right, just like this." Bud propped the handle of the frying pan high with a forked stick, and stood up. "Say, my name's Bud Moore, and I'm not headed anywhere in particular. I'm just traveling in one general direction, and that's with the Coast at my back. Drifting, that's all. I ain't done anything I'm ashamed of or scared of, but I am kinda bashful about towns. I tangled with a couple of crooks, and they're pulled by now, I expect. I'm dodging newspaper notoriety. Don't want to be named with 'em at all." He, spread his hands with an air of finality. "That's my tale of woe," he supplemented, "boiled down to essentials. I just thought I'd tell you."

"Yeah. Well, my name's Cash Markham, and I despise to have folks get funny over it. I'm a miner and prospector, and I'm outfitting for a trip for another party, looking up an old location that showed good prospects ten years ago. Man died, and his wife's trying to get the claim relocated. Get you a plate outa that furtherest kyack, and a cup. Bannock looks about done, so we'll eat."

That night Bud shared Cash Markham's blankets, and in the morning he cooked the breakfast while Cash Markham rounded up the burros and horses. In that freemasonry of the wilderness they dispensed with credentials, save those each man carried in his face and in his manner. And if you stop to think of it, such credentials are not easily forged, for nature writes them down, and nature is a truth-loving old dame who will never lead you far astray if only she is left alone to do her work in peace.

It transpired, in the course of the forenoon's travel, that Cash Markham would like to have a partner, if he could find a man that suited. One guessed that he was fastidious in the matter of choosing his companions, in spite of the easy way in which he had accepted Bud. By noon they had agreed that Bud should go along and help relocate the widow's claim. Cash Markham hinted that they might do a little prospecting on their own account. It was a country he had long wanted to get into, he said, and while he intended to do what Mrs. Thompson had hired him to do, still there was no law against their prospecting on their own account. And that, he explained, was one reason why he wanted a good man along. If the Thompson claim was there, Bud could do the work under the supervision of Cash, and Cash could prospect.

"And anyway, it's bad policy for a man to go off alone in this part of the country," he added with a speculative look across the sandy waste they were skirting at a pace to suit the heavily packed burros. "Case of sickness or accident—or suppose the stock strays off—it's bad to be alone."

"Suits me fine to go with you," Bud declared. "I'm next thing to broke, but I've got a lot of muscle I can cash in on the deal. And I know the open. And I can rock a gold-pan and not spill out all the colors, if there is any—and whatever else I know is liable to come in handy, and what I don't know I can learn."

"That's fair enough. Fair enough," Markham agreed. "I'll allow you wages on the Thompson job' till you've earned enough to balance up with the outfit. After that it'll be fifty-fifty. How'll that be, Bud?"

"Fair enough—fair enough," Bud retorted with faint mimicry. "If I was all up in the air a few days ago, I seem to have lit on my feet, and that's good enough for me right now. We'll let 'er ride that way."

And the twinkle, as he talked, was back in his eyes, and the smiley quirk was at the corner of his lips.

CHAPTER SEVEN.

INTO THE DESERT

If you want to know what mad adventure Bud found himself launched upon, just read a few extracts from the diary which Cash Markham, being a methodical sort of person, kept faithfully from day to day, until he cut his thumb on a can of tomatoes which he had been cutting open with his knife. After that Bud kept the diary for him, jotting down the main happenings of the day. When Cash's thumb healed so that he could hold a pencil with some comfort, Bud thankfully relinquished the task. He hated to write, anyway, and it seemed to him that Cash ought to trust his memory a little more than he did.

I shall skip a good many days, of course—though the diary did not, I assure you.

First, there was the outfit. When they had outfitted at Needles for the real trip, Cash set down the names of all living things in this wise:

Outfit, Cassius B. Markham, Bud Moore, Daddy a bull terrier, bay horse, Mars, Pete a sorrel, Ed a burro, Swayback a jinny, Maude a jack, Cora another jinny, Billy a riding burro & Sways colt & Maude colt a white mean looking little devil.

Sat. Apr. 1.

Up at 7:30. Snowing and blowing 3 ft. of snow on ground. Managed to get breakfast & returned to bed. Fed Monte & Peter our cornmeal, poor things half frozen. Made a fire in tent at 1:30 & cooked a meal. Much smoke, ripped hole in back of tent. Three burros in sight weathering fairly well. No sign of let up everything under snow & wind a gale. Making out fairly well under adverse conditions. Worst weather we have experienced.

Apr. 2.

Up at 7 A.M. Fine & sunny snow going fast. Fixed up tent & cleaned up generally. Alkali flat a lake, can't cross till it dries. Stock some scattered, brought them all together.

Apr. 3.

Up 7 A.M. Clear & bright. Snow going fast. All creeks flowing. Fine sunny day.

Apr. 4.

Up 6 A.M. Clear & bright. Went up on divide, met 3 punchers who said road impassable. Saw 2 trains stalled away across alkali flat. Very boggy and moist.

Apr.5.

Up 5 A.M. Clear & bright. Start out, on Monte & Pete at 6. Animals traveled well, did not appear tired. Feed fine all over. Plenty water everywhere.

Not much like Bud's auto stage, was it? But the very novelty of it, the harking back to old plains days, appealed to him and sent him forward from dull hardship to duller discomfort, and kept the quirk at the corners of his lips and the twinkle in his eyes. Bud liked to travel this way, though it took them all day long to cover as much distance as he had been wont to slide behind him in an hour. He liked it—this slow, monotonous journeying across the lean land which Cash had traversed years ago, where the stark, black pinnacles and rough knobs of rock might be hiding Indians with good eyesight and a vindictive temperament. Cash told him many things out of his past, while they poked along, driving the packed burros before them. Things which he never had set down in his diary—things which he did not tell to any one save his few friends.

But it was not always mud and rain and snow, as Cash's meager chronicle betrays.

May 6.

Up at sunrise. Monte & Pete gone leaving no tracks. Bud found them 3 miles South near Indian village. Bud cut his hair, did a good job. Prospector dropped into camp with fist full of good looking quartz. Stock very thirsty all day. Very hot Tied Monte & Pete up for night.

May 8.

Up 5:30. Fine, but hot. Left 7:30. Pete walked over a sidewinder & Bud shot him ten ft. in air. Also prior killed another beside road. Feed as usual, desert weeds. Pulled grain growing side of track and fed plugs. Water from cistern & R.R. ties for fuel. Put up tent for shade. Flies horrible.

May 9.

Up 4. Left 6. Feed as usual. Killed a sidewinder in a bush with 3 shots of Krag. Made 21 m. today. R.R. ties for fuel Cool breeze all day.

May 11.

Up at sunrise. Bud washed clothes. Tested rock. Fine looking mineral country here. Dressed Monte's withers with liniment greatly reducing swelling from saddle-gall. He likes to have it dressed & came of his own accord. Day quite comfortable.

May 15.

Up 4. Left 6:30 over desert plain & up dry wash. Daddy suffered from heat & ran into cactus while looking for shade. Got it in his mouth, tongue, feet & all over body. Fixed him up poor creature groaned all evening & would not eat his supper. Poor feed & wood here. Water found by digging 2 ft. in sand in sandstone basins in bed of dry wash. Monte lay down en route. Very hot & all suffered from heat.

May 16.

Bud has sick headache. Very hot so laid around camp all day. Put two blankets up on tent pols for sun break. Daddy under weather from cactus experience. Papago Indian boy about 18 on fine bay mare driving 4 ponies watered at our well. Moon almost full, lots of mocking birds. Pretty songs.

May 17.

Up 7:30 Bud some better. Day promises hot, but slight breeze. White gauzy clouds in sky. Daddy better. Monte & Pete gone all day. Hunted twice but impossible to track them in this stony soil Bud followed trail, found them 2 mi. east of here in flat sound asleep about 3 P.M. At 6 went to flat 1/4 mi. N. of camp to tie Pete, leading Monte by bell strap almost stepped on rattler 3 ft. long. 10 rattles & a button. Killed him. To date, 1 Prairie rattler, 3 Diamond back & 8 sidewinders, 12 in all. Bud feels better.

May 18.

At 4 A. M. Bud woke up by stock passing camp. Spoke to me who half awake hollered, "sic Daddy!" Daddy sicced 'em & they went up bank of wash to right. Bud swore it was Monte & Pete. I went to flat & found M. & P. safe. Water in sink all gone. Bud got stomach trouble. I threw up my breakfast. Very hot weather. Lanced Monte's back & dressed it with creoline. Turned them loose & away they put again.

Soon after this they arrived at the place where Thompson had located his claim. It was desert, of course, sloping away on one side to a dreary waste of sand and weeds with now and then a giant cactus standing gloomily alone with malformed lingers stretched stiffly to the staring blue sky. Behind where they pitched their final camp—Camp 48, Cash Markham recorded it in his diary—the hills rose. But they were as stark and barren almost as the desert below. Black rock humps here and there, with ledges of mineral bearing rock. Bushes and weeds and dry washes for the rest, with enough struggling grass to feed the horses and burros if they rustled hard enough for it.

They settled down quietly to a life of grinding monotony that would have driven some men crazy. But Bud, because it was a man's kind of monotony, bore it cheerfully. He was out of doors, and he was hedged about by no rules or petty restrictions. He liked Cash Markham and he liked Pete, his saddle horse, and he was fond of Daddy who was still paying the penalty of seeking too carelessly for shade and, according to Cash's record, "getting it in his mouth, tongue, feet & all over body." Bud liked it—all except the blistering heat and the "side-winders" and other rattlers. He did not bother with trying to formulate any explanation of why he liked it. It may have been picturesque, though picturesqueness of that sort is better appreciated when it is seen through the dim radiance of memory that blurs sordid details. Certainly it was not adventurous, as men have come to judge adventure.

Life droned along very dully. Day after day was filled with petty details. A hill looks like a mountain if it rises abruptly out of a level plain, with no real mountains in sight to measure it by. Here's the diary to prove how little things came to look important because the days held no contrasts. If it bores you to read it, think what it must have been to live it.

June 10.

Up at 6:30 Baked till 11. Then unrigged well and rigged up an incline for the stock to water. Bud dressed Daddy's back. Stock did not come in all morning, but Monte & Pete came in before supper. Incline water shaft does not work. Prospected & found 8 ledges. Bud found none.

June 11.

After breakfast fixed up shack—shelves, benches, tools, etc. Cleaned guns. Bud dressed Daddy's back which is much better. Strong gold in test of ledge, I found below creek. Took more specimens to sample. Cora comes in with a little black colt newly born. Proud as a bull pup with two tails. Monte & Pete did not come in so we went by lantern light a mile or so down the wash & found them headed this way & snake them in to drink about 80 gallons of water apiece. Daddy tied up and howling like a demon all the while. Bud took a bath.

June 12.

Bud got out and got breakfast again. Then started off on Pete to hunt trail that makes short cut 18 miles to Bend. Roofed the kitchen. Bud got back about 1:30, being gone 6 hours. Found trail & two good ledges. Cora & colt came for water. Other burros did not. Brought in specimens from ledge up creek that showed very rich gold in tests. Burros came in at 9:30. Bud got up and tied them up.

June 13.

Bud gets breakfast. I took Sway & brought in load of wood. Bud went out and found a wash lined with good looking ledges. Hung up white rags on bushes to identify same. Found large ledge of good quartz showing fine in tests about one mile down wash. Bud dressed Daddy's back. Located a claim west of Thompson's. Burros did not come in except Cora & colt. Pete & Monte came separated.

June 14.

Bud got breakfast & dressed Daddy's back. Very hot day. Stock came in about 2. Tied up Billy Maud & Cora. Bud has had headache. Monte & Pete did not come in. Bud went after them & found them 4 miles away where we killed the Gila monster. Sent 2 samples from big ledge to Tucson for assay. Daddy better.

June 15.

Up 2.30. Bud left for Bend at 4. Walked down to flat but could not see stock. About 3 Cora & Colt came in for water & Sway & Ed from the south about 5. No Monte. Monte got in about midnight & went past kitchen to creek on run. Got up, found him very nervous & frightened & tied him up.

June 17.

Bud got back 4 P.M. in gale of wind & sand. Burros did not come in for water. Very hot. Bud brought canned stuff. Rigged gallows for No. 2 shaft also block & tackle & pail for drinking water, also washed clothes. While drying went around in cap undershirt & shoes.

June 18.

Burros came in during night for water. Hot as nether depths of infernal regions. Went up on hill a mile away. Seamed with veins similar to shaft No. 2 ore. Blew in two faces & got good looking ore seamed with a black incrustation, oxide of something, but what could not determine. Could find neither silver nor copper in it. Monte & Pete came in about 1 & tied them up. Very hot. Hottest day yet, even the breeze scorching. Test of ore showed best yet. One half of solution in tube turning to chloride of gold, 3 tests showing same. Burros except Ed & Cora do not come in days any more. Bud made a gate for kitchen to keep burros out.

The next morning it was that Cash cut the ball of his right thumb open on the sharp edge of a tomato can. He wanted the diary to go on as usual. He had promised, he said, to keep one for the widow who wanted a record of the way the work was carried on, and the progress made. Bud could not see that there had been much progress, except as a matter of miles. Put a speedometer on one of his legs, he told Cash, and he'd bet it would register more mileage chasing after them fool burros than his auto stage could show after a full season. As for working the widow's claim, it was not worth working, from all he could judge of it. And if it were full of gold as the United States treasury, the burros took up all their time so they couldn't do much. Between doggone stock drinking or not drinking and the darn fool diary that had to be kept, Bud opined that they needed an extra hand or two. Bud was peevish, these days. Gila Bend had exasperated him because it was not the town it called itself, but a huddle of adobe huts. He had come away in the sour mood of a thirsty man who finds an alkali spring sparkling deceptively under a rock. Furthermore, the nights had been hot and the mosquitoes a humming torment. And as a last affliction he was called upon to keep the diary going. He did it, faithfully enough but in a fashion of his own.

First he read back a few pages to get the hang of the thing. Then he shook down Cash's fountain pen, that dried quickly in that heat. Then he read another page as a model, and wrote:

June 19.

Mosquitoes last night was worse than the heat and that was worse than Gila Bend's great white way. Hunted up the burros. Pete and Monte came in and drank. Monte had colic. We fed them and turned them loose but the blamed fools hung around all day and eat up some sour beans I throwed out. Cash was peeved and swore they couldn't have another grain of feed. But Monte come to the shack and watched Cash through a knothole the size of one eye till Cash opened up his heart and the bag. Cash cut his thumb opening tomatoes. The tomatoes wasn't hurt any.

June 20.

Got breakfast. Bill and harem did not come to water. Cash done the regular hike after them. His thumb don't hurt him for hazing donkeys. Bill and harem come in after Cash left. They must of saw him go. Cash was out four hours and come in mad. Shot a hidrophobia skunk out by the creek. Nothing doing. Too hot.

June 21.

The sun would blister a mud turtle so he'd holler. Cash put in most of day holding a parasol over his garden patch. Burros did not miss their daily drink. Night brings mosquitoes with their wings singed but their stingers O.K. They must hole up daytimes or they would fry.

June 22.

Thought I know what heat was. I never did before. Cash took a bath. It was his first. Burros did not come to water. Cash and I tried to sleep on kitchen roof but the darned mosquitoes fed up on us and then played heavenly choir all night.

June 25.

Cash got back from Bend. Thumb is better and he can have this job any time now. He hustled up a widow that made a couple of mosquito bags to go over our heads. No shape (bags, not widow) but help keep flies and mosquitoes from chewing on us all day and all night. Training for hades. I can stand the heat as well as the old boy with the pitch-fork. Ain't got used to brimstone yet, but I'd trade mosquitoes for sulphur smoke and give some boot. Worried about Cash. He took a bath today again, using water I had packed for mine. Heat must be getting him.

June 26.

Cash opened up thumb again, trying to brain Pete with rock. Pete got halfway into kitchen and eat biggest part of a pie I made. Cash threw jagged rock, hit Pete in side of jaw. Cut big gash. Swelled now like a punkin. Cash and I tangled over same. I'm going to quit. I have had enough of this darn country. Creek's drying up, and mosquitoes have found way to crawl under bags. Cash wants me to stay till we find good claim, but Cash can go to thunder.

Then Cash's record goes on:

June 27.

Bud very sick & out of head. Think it is heat, which is terrible. Talked all night about burros, gasoline, & camphor balls which he seemed wanting to buy in gunny sack. No sleep for either. Burros came in for water about daylight. Picketed Monte & Pete as may need doctor if Bud grows worse. Thumb nearly well.

June 27.

Bud same, slept most of day. Gave liver pills & made gruel of cornmeal, best could do with present stores. Burros came at about 3 but could not drink owing to bees around water hold. Monte got stung and kicked over water cans & buckets I had salted for burros. Burros put for hills again. No way of driving off bees.

June 28.

Burros came & drank in night. Cooler breeze, Bud some better & slept. Sway has badly swollen neck. May be rattler bite or perhaps bee. Bud wanted cigarettes but smoked last the day before he took sick. Gave him more liver pills & sponge off with water every hour. Best can do under circumstances. Have not prospected account Bud's sickness.

June 29.

Very hot all day, breeze like blast from furnace. Burros refuse to leave flat.

Bees better, as can't fly well in this wind. Bud worse. High fever & very restless & flighty. Imagines much trouble with automobile, talk very technical & can't make head or tail of it. Monte & Pete did not come in, left soon as turned loose. No feed for them here & figured Bud too sick to travel or stay alone so horses useless at present. Sponged frequently with coolest water can get, seems to give some relief as he is quieter afterwards.

July 4th.

Monte & Pete came in the night & hung around all day. Drove them away from vicinity of shack several times but they returned & moped in shade of house. Terrible hot, strong gusty wind. Bud sat up part of day, slept rest of time. Looks very thin and great hollows under eyes, but chief trouble seems to be, no cigarettes. Shade over radishes & lettice works all right. Watered copiously at daylight & again at dusk. Doing fine. Fixed fence which M & P. broke down while tramping around. Prospected west of ranche. Found enormous ledge of black quartz, looks like sulphur stem during volcanic era but may be iron. Strong gold & heavy precipitate in test, silver test poor but on filtering showed like white of egg in tube (unusual). Clearing iron out showed for gold the highest yet made, being more pronounced with Fenosulphate than $1500 rock have seen. Immense ledge of it & slightest estimate from test at least $10. Did not tell Bud as keeping for surprise when he is able to visit ledge. Very monotonous since Bud has been sick. Bud woke up & said Hell of a Fourth & turned over & went to sleep again with mosquito net over head to keep off flies. Burros came in after dark, all but Cora & Colt, which arrived about midnight. Daddy gone since yesterday morning leaving no trace.

July 5.

Miserable hot night. Burros trickled in sometime during night. Bud better, managed to walk to big ledge after sundown. Suggests we call it the Burro Lode. His idea of wit, claims we have occupied camp all summer for sake of timing burros when they come to waterhole. Wish to call it Columbia mine for patriotic reasons having found it on Fourth. Will settle it soon so as to put up location. Put in 2 shots & pulpel samples for assay. Rigged windows on shack to keep out bees, nats & flies & mosquitoes. Bud objects because it keeps out air as well. Took them off. Sick folks must be humored. Hot, miserable and sleepless. Bud very restless.

July 6.

Cool wind makes weather endurable, but bees terrible in kitchen & around water-hole. Flipped a dollar to settle name of big ledge. Bud won tails, Burro lode. Must cultivate my sense of humor so as to see the joke. Bud agrees to stay & help develop claim. Still very weak, puttered around house all day cleaning & baking bread & stewing fruit which brought bees by millions so we could not eat same till after dark when they subsided. Bud got stung twice in kitchen. Very peevish & full of cuss. Says positively must make trip to Bend & get cigarettes tomorrow or will blow up whole outfit. Has already blowed up same several times today with no damage. Burros came in about 5. Monte & Pete later, tied them up with grain. Pete has very bad eye. Bud will ride Monte if not too hot for trip. Still no sign of daddy, think must be dead or stolen though nobody to steal same in country.

July 7.

Put in 2 shots on Burro Lode & got her down to required depth. Hot. Bud finds old location on widow's claim, upturns all previous calculation & information given me by her. Wrote letter explaining same, which Bud will mail. Bud left 4 P.M. should make Bend by midnight. Much better but still weak Burros came in late & hung around water hole. Put up monument at Burro Lode. Sent off samples to assay at Tucson. Killed rattler near shack, making 16 so far killed.

CHAPTER EIGHT.
MANY BARREN MONTHS AND MILES

"Well, here come them darn burros, Cash. Cora's colt ain't with 'em though. Poor little devils—say, Cash, they look like hard sleddin', and that's a fact. I'll tell the world they've got about as much pep as a flat tire."

"Maybe we better grain 'em again." Cash looked up from studying the last assay report of the Burro Lode, and his look was not pleasant. "But it'll cost a good deal, in both time and money. The feed around here is played out."

"Well, when it comes to that—" Bud cast a glum glance at the paper Cash was holding.

"Yeah. Looks like everything's about played out. Promising ledge, too. Like some people, though. Most all its good points is right on the surface. Nothing to back it up."

"She's sure running light, all right. Now," Bud added sardonically, but with the whimsical quirk withal, "if it was like a carburetor, and you could give it a richer mixture—"

"Yeah. What do you make of it, Bud?"

"Well—aw, there comes that durn colt, bringing up the drag. Say Cash, that colt's just about all in. Cora's nothing but a bag of bones, too. They'll never winter—not on this range, they won't."

Cash got up and went to the doorway, looking out over Bud's shoulder at the spiritless donkeys trailing in to water. Beyond them the desert baked in its rim of hot, treeless hills. Above them the sky glared a brassy blue with never a could. Over a low ridge came Monte and Pete, walking with heads drooping. Their hip bones lifted above their ridged paunches, their backbones, peaked sharp above, their withers were lean and pinched looking. In August the desert herbage has lost what little succulence it ever possessed, and the gleanings are scarce worth the walking after.

"They're pretty thin," Cash observed speculatively, as though he was measuring them mentally for some particular need.

"We'd have to grain 'em heavy till we struck better feed. And pack light." Bud answered his thought.

"The question is, where shall we head for, Bud? Have you any particular idea?" Cash looked slightingly down at the assayer's report. "Such as she is, we've done all we can do to the Burro Lode, for a year at least," he said. "The assessment work is all done—or will be when we muck out after that last shot. The claim is filed—I don't know what more we can do right away. Do you?"

"Sure thing," grinned Bud. "We can get outa here and go some place where it's green."

"Yeah." Cash meditated, absently eyeing the burros. "Where it's green." He looked at the near hills, and at the desert, and at the dreary march of the starved animals. "It's a long way to green country," he said.

They looked at the burros.

"They're tough little devils," Bud observed hopefully. "We could take it easy, traveling when it's coolest. And by packing light, and graining the whole bunch—"

"Yeah. We can ease 'em through, I guess. It does seem as though it would be foolish to hang on here any longer." Carefully as he made his tests, Cash weighed the question of their going. "This last report kills any chance of interesting capital to the extent of developing the claim on a large enough scale to make it profitable. It's too long a haul to take the ore out, and it's too spotted to justify any great investment in machinery to handle it on the ground. And," he added with an undernote of fierceness, "it's a terrible place for man or beast to stay in, unless the object to be attained is great enough to justify enduring the hardships."

"You said a mouthful, Cash. Well, can you leave your seven radishes and three hunches of lettuce and pull out—say at daybreak?" Bud turned to him with some eagerness.

Cash grinned sourly. "When it's time to go, seven radishes can't stop me. No, nor a whole row of 'em—if there was a whole row."

"And you watered 'em copiously too," Bud murmured, with the corners of his mouth twitching. "Well, I guess we might as well tie up the livestock. I'm going to give 'em all a feed of rolled oats, Cash. We can get along without, and they've got to have something to put a little heart in 'em. There's a moon to-night—how about starting along about midnight? That would put us in the Bend early in the forenoon to-morrow."

"Suits me," said Cash. "Now I've made up my mind about going, I can't go too soon."

"You're on. Midnight sees us started." Bud went out with ropes to catch and tie up the burros and their two saddle horses. And as he went, for the first time in two months he whistled; a detail which Cash noted with a queer kind of smile.

Midnight and the moon riding high in the purple bowl of sky sprinkled thick with stars; with a little, warm wind stirring the parched weeds as they passed; with the burros shuffling single file along the dim trail which was the short cut through the hills to the Bend, Ed taking the lead, with the camp kitchen wabbling lumpily on his back, Cora bringing up the rear with her skinny colt trying its best to keep up, and with no pack at all; so they started on the long, long journey to the green country.

A silent journey it was for the most part. The moon and the starry bowl of sky had laid their spell upon the desert, and the two men rode wordlessly, filled with vague, unreasoning regret that they must go. Months they had spent with the desert, learning well every little varying mood; cursing it for its blistering heat and its sand storms and its parched thirst and its utter, blank loneliness. Loving it too, without ever dreaming that they loved. To-morrow they would face the future with the past dropping farther and farther behind. To-night it rode with them.

Three months in that little, rough-walled hut had lent it an atmosphere of home, which a man instinctively responds to with a certain clinging affection, however crude may be the shelter he calls his own. Cash secretly regretted the thirsty death of his radishes and lettuce which he had planted and tended with such optimistic care. Bud wondered if Daddy might not stray half-starved into the shack, and find them gone. While they were there, he had agreed with Cash that the dog must be dead. But now he felt uneasily doubtful It would be fierce if Daddy did come back now. He would starve. He never could make the trip to the Bend alone, even if he could track them.

There was, also, the disappointment in the Burro Lode claim. As Bud planned it, the Burro was packing a very light load—far lighter than had seemed possible with that strong indication on the surface. Cash's "enormous black ledge" had shown less and less gold as they went into it, though it still seemed worth while, if they had the capital to develop it further. Wherefore they had done generous assessment work and had recorded their claim and built their monuments to mark its boundaries. It would be safe for a year, and by that time—Quien sabe?

The Thompson claim, too, had not justified any enthusiasm whatever. They had found it, had relocated it, and worked out the assessment for the widow. Cash had her check for all they had earned, and he had declared profanely that he would not give his share of the check for the whole claim.

They would go on prospecting, using the check for a grubstake, That much they had decided without argument. The gambling instinct was wide awake in Bud's nature—and as for Cash, he would hunt gold as long as he could carry pick and pan. They would prospect as long as their money held out. When that was gone, they would get more and go on prospecting. But they would prospect in a green country where wood and water were not so precious as in the desert and where, Cash averred, the chance of striking it rich was just as good; better, because they could kill game and make their grubstake last longer.

Wherefore they waited in Gila Bend for three days, to strengthen the weak-ened animals with rest and good hay and grain. Then they took again to the trail, traveling as lightly as they could, with food for themselves and grain for the stock to last them until they reached Needles. From there with fresh supplies they pushed on up to Goldfield, found that camp in the throes of labor disputes, and went on to Tonopah.

There they found work for themselves and the burros, packing winter sup-plies to a mine lying back in the hills. They made money at it, and during the winter they made more. With the opening of spring they outfitted again and took the trail, their goal the high mountains south of Honey Lake. They did not hurry. Wherever the land they traveled through seemed to promise gold, they would stop and prospect. Many a pan of likely looking dirt they washed beside some stream where the burros stopped to drink and feed a little on the grassy banks.

So, late in June, they reached Reno; outfitted and went on again, traveling to the north, to the green country for which they yearned, though now they were fairly in it and would have stopped if any tempting ledge or bar had come in their way. They prospected every gulch that showed any mineral signs at all. It was a carefree kind of life, with just enough of variety to hold Bud's interest to the adventuring. The nomad in him responded easily to this leisurely pilgrimage. There was no stampede anywhere to stir their blood with the thought of quick wealth. There was hope enough, on the other hand, to keep them going. Cash had prospected and trapped for more than fifteen years now, and he preached the doctrine of freedom and the great outdoors.

Of what use was a house and lot—and taxes and trouble with the plumbing? he would chuckle. A tent and blankets and a frying pan and grub; two good legs and wild country to travel; a gold pan and a pick—these things, to Cash, spelled independence and the joy of living. The burros and the two horses were luxuries, he declared. When they once got located on a good claim they would sell off everything but a couple of burros—Sway and Ed, most likely. The others would bring enough for a winter grubstake, and would prolong their freedom and their independence just that much. That is, supposing they did not strike a good claim before then. Cash had learned, he said, to hope high but keep an eye on the grubstake.

Late in August they came upon a mountain village perched beside a swift stream and walled in on three sided by pine-covered mountains. A branch railroad linked the place more or less precariously with civilization, and every day—unless there was a washout somewhere, or a snowslide, or drifts too deep—a train passed over the road. One day it would go up-stream, and the next day it would come back. And the houses stood drawn up in a row alongside the track to watch for these passings.

Miners came in with burros or with horses, packed flour and bacon and tea and coffee across their middles, got drunk, perhaps as a parting ceremony, and went away into the hills. Cash watched them for a day or so; saw the size of their grubstakes, asked few questions and listened to a good deal of small-town gossip, and nodded his head contentedly. There was gold in these hills. Not enough, perhaps, to start a stampede with—but enough to keep wise old hermits burrowing after it.

So one day Bud sold the two horses and one of the saddles, and Cash bought flour and bacon and beans and coffee, and added other things quite as desirable but not so necessary. Then they too went away into the hills.

Fifteen miles from Alpine, as a cannon would shoot; high up in the hills, where a creek flowed down through a saucerlike basin under beetling ledges fringed all around with forest, they came, after much wandering, upon an old log cabin whose dirt roof still held in spite of the snows that heaped upon it through many a winter. The ledge showed the scars of old prospect holes, and in the sand of the creek they found "colors" strong enough to make it seem worth while to stop here—for awhile, at least.

They cleaned out the cabin and took possession of it, and the next time they went to town Cash made cautious inquiries about the place. It was, he learned, an old abandoned claim. Abandoned chiefly because the old miner who had lived there died one day, and left behind him all the marks of having died from starvation, mostly. A cursory examination of his few belongings had revealed much want, but no gold save a little coarse dust in a small bottle.

"About enough to fill a rifle ca'tridge," detailed the teller of the tale. "He'd pecked around that draw for two, three year mebby. Never showed no gold much, for all the time he spent there. Trapped some in winter—coyotes and bobcats and skunks, mostly. Kinda off in the upper story, old Nelson was. I guess he just stayed there because he happened to light there and didn't have gumption enough to git out. Hills is full of old fellers like him. They live off to the'rselves, and peck around and git a pocket now and then that keeps 'm in grub and tobacco. If you want to use the cabin, I guess nobody's goin' to care. Nelson never had any folks, that anybody knows of. Nobody ever bothered about takin' up the claim after he cashed in, either. Didn't seem worth nothin' much. Went back to the gov'ment."

"Trapped, you say. Any game around there now?"

"Oh, shore! Game everywhere in these hills, from weasels up to bear and mountain lion. If you want to trap, that's as good a place as any, I guess."

So Cash and Bud sold the burros and bought traps and more supplies, and two window sashes and a crosscut saw and some wedges and a double-bitted axe, and settled down in Nelson Flat to find what old Dame Fortune had tucked away in this little side pocket and forgotten.

CHAPTER NINE.
THE BITE OF MEMORY

The heavy boom of a dynamite blast rolled across the fiat to the hills that flung it back in a tardy echo like a spent ball of sound. A blob of blue smoke curled out of a hole the size of a hogshead in a steep bank overhung with alders. Outside, the wind caught the smoke and carried streamers of it away to play with. A startled bluejay, on a limb high up on the bank, lifted his slaty crest and teetered forward, clinging with his toe nails to the branch while he scolded down at the men who had scared him so. A rattle of clods and small rocks fell from their high flight into the sweet air of a mountain sunset.

"Good execution, that was," Cash remarked, craning his neck toward the hole. "If you're a mind to go on ahead and cook supper, I'll stay and see if we opened up anything. Or you can stay, just as you please."

Dynamite smoke invariably made Bud's head ache splittingly. Cash was not so susceptible. Bud chose the cooking, and went away down the flat, the bluejay screaming insults after him. He was frying bacon when Cash came in, a hatful of broken rock riding in the hollow of his arm.

"Got something pretty good here, Bud—if she don't turn out like that dang Burro Lode ledge. Look here. Best looking quartz we've struck yet. What do you think of it?"

He dumped the rock out on the oilcloth behind the sugar can and directly under the little square window through which the sun was pouring a lavish yellow flood of light before it dropped behind the peak. Bud set the bacon back where it would not burn, and bent over the table to look.

"Gee, but it's heavy!" he cried, picking up a fragment the size of an egg, and balancing it in his hands. "I don't know a lot about gold-bearing quartz, but she looks good to me, all right."

"Yeah. It is good, unless I'm badly mistaken. I'll test some after supper. Old Nelson couldn't have used powder at all, or he'd have uncovered enough of this, I should think, to show the rest what he had. Or maybe he died just when he had started that hole. Seems queer he never struck pay dirt in this flat. Well, let's eat if it's ready, Bud. Then we'll see."

"Seems kinda queer, don't it, Cash, that nobody stepped in and filed on any claims here?" Bud dumped half a kettle of boiled beans into a basin and set it on the table. "Want any prunes to-night, Cash?"

Cash did not want prunes, which was just as well, seeing there were none cooked. He sat down and ate, with his mind and his eyes clinging to the grayish, veined fragments of rock lying on the table beside his plate.

"We'll send some of that down to Sacramento right away," he observed, "and have it assayed. And we won't let out anything about it, Bud — good or bad. I like this flat. I don't want it mucked over with a lot of gold-crazy lunatics."

Bud laughed and reached for the bacon. "We ain't been followed up with stampedes so far," he pointed out. "Burro Lode never caused a ripple in the Bend, you recollect. And I'll tell a sinful world it looked awful good, too."

"Yeah. Well, Arizona's hard to excite. They've had so dang much strenuosity all their lives, and then the climate's against violent effort, either mental or physical. I was calm, perfectly calm when I discovered that big ledge. It is just as well — seeing how it petered out."

"What'll you bet this pans out the same?"

"I never bet. No one but a fool will gamble." Cash pressed his lips together in a way that drove the color from there.

"Oh, yuh don't! Say, you're the king bee of all gamblers. Been prospecting for fifteen years, according to you — and then you've got the nerve to say you don't gamble!"

Cash ignored the charge. He picked up a piece of rock and held it to the fading light. "It looks good," he said again. "Better than that placer ground down by the creek. That's all right, too. We can wash enough gold there to keep us going while we develop this. That is, if this proves as good as it looks."

Bud looked across at him enigmatically. "Well, here's hoping she's worth a million. You go ahead with your tests, Cash. I'll wash the dishes."

"Of course," Cash began to conserve his enthusiasm, "there's nothing so sure as an assay. And it was too dark in the hole to see how much was uncovered. This may be just a freak deposit. There may not be any real vein of it. You can't tell until it's developed further. But it looks good. Awful good."

His makeshift tests confirmed his opinion. Bud started out next day with three different samples for the assayer, and an air castle or two to keep him company. He would like to find himself half owner of a mine worth about a million, he mused. Maybe Marie would wish then that she had thought twice about quitting him just on her mother's say-so. He'd like to go buzzing into San Jose behind the wheel of a car like the one Foster had fooled him into stealing. And meet Marie, and her mother too, and let them get an eyeful. He guessed the old lady would have to swallow what she had said about him being lazy — just because he couldn't run an auto-stage in the winter to Big Basin! What was the matter with the old woman, anyway? Didn't he keep Maria in comfort. Well, he'd like to see her face when he drove along the street in a big new Sussex. She'd wish she had let him and Marie alone. They would have made out all right if they had been let alone. He ought to have taken Marie to some other town, where her mother couldn't nag at her every day about him. Marie wasn't such a bad kid, if she were left alone. They might have been happy—

He tried then to shake himself free of thoughts of her. That was the trouble with him, he brooded morosely. He couldn't let his thoughts ride free, any more. They kept heading straight for Marie. He could not see why she should cling so to his memory; he had not wronged her—unless it was by letting her go without making a bigger fight for their home. Still, she had gone of her own free will. He was the one that had been wronged—why, hadn't they lied about him in court and to the gossipy neighbors? Hadn't they broke him? No. If the mine panned out big as Cash seemed to think was likely, the best thing he could do was steer clear of San Jose. And whether it panned out or not, the best thing he could do was forget that such girl as Marie had ever existed..

Which was all very well, as far as it went. The trouble was that resolving not to think of Marie, calling up all the bitterness he could muster against her memory, did no more toward blotting her image from his mind than did the miles and the months he had put between them.

He reached the town in a dour mood of unrest, spite of the promise of wealth he carried in his pocket. He mailed the package and the letter, and went to a saloon and had a highball. He was not a drinking man—at least, he never had been one, beyond a convivial glass or two with his fellows—but he felt that day the need of a little push toward optimism. In the back part of the room three men were playing freeze-out. Bud went over and stood with his hands in his pockets and watched them, because there was nothing else to do, and because he was still having some trouble with his thoughts. He was lonely, without quite knowing what ailed him. He hungered for friends to hail him with that cordial, "Hello, Bud!" when they saw him coming.

No one in Alpine had said hello, Bud, when he came walking in that day. The postmaster had given him one measuring glance when he had weighed the package of ore, but he had not spoken except to name the amount of postage required. The bartender had made some remark about the weather, and had smiled with a surface friendliness that did not deceive Bud for a moment. He knew too well that the smile was not for him, but for his patronage.

He watched the game. And when the man opposite him pushed back his chair and, looking up at Bud, asked if he wanted to sit in, Bud went and sat down, buying a dollar's worth of chips as an evidence of his intention to play. His interest in the game was not keen. He played for the feeling it gave him of being one of the bunch, a man among his friends; or if not friends, at least acquaintances. And, such was his varying luck with the cards, he played for an hour or so without having won enough to irritate his companions. Wherefore he rose from the table at supper time calling one young fellow Frank quite naturally. They went to the Alpine House and had supper together, and after that they sat in the office and talked about automobiles for an hour, which gave Bud a comforting sense of having fallen among friends.

Later they strolled over to a picture show which ran films two years behind their first release, and charged fifteen cents for the privilege of watching them. It was the first theater Bud had entered since he left San Jose, and at the last minute he hesitated, tempted to turn back. He hated moving pictures. They always had love scenes somewhere in the story, and love scenes hurt. But Frank had already bought two tickets, and it seemed unfriendly to turn back now. He went inside to the jangling of a player-piano in dire need of a tuner's service, and sat down near the back of the hall with his hat upon his lifted knees which could have used more space between the seats.

While they waited for the program they talked in low tones, a mumble of commonplaces. Bud forgot for the moment his distaste for such places, and let himself slip easily back into the old thought channels, the old habits of relaxation after a day's work was done. He laughed at the one-reel comedy that had for its climax a chase of housemaids, policemen, and outraged fruit vendors after a well-meaning but unfortunate lover. He saw the lover pulled ignominiously out of a duck pond and soused relentlessly into a watering trough, and laughed with Frank and called it some picture.

He eyed a succession of "current events" long since gone stale out where the world moved swifter than here in the mountains, and he felt as though he had come once more into close touch with life. All the dull months he had spent with Cash and the burros dwarfed into a pointless, irrelevant incident of his life. He felt that he ought to be out in the world, doing bigger things than hunting gold that somehow always refused at the last minute to be found. He stirred restlessly. He was free—there was nothing to hold him if he wanted to go. The war—he believed he would go over and take a hand. He could drive an ambulance or a truck—

Current Events, however, came abruptly to an end; and presently Bud's vagrant, half-formed desire for achievement merged into biting recollections. Here was a love drama, three reels of it. At first Bud watched it with only a vague, disquieting sense of familiarity. Then abruptly he recalled too vividly the time and circumstance of his first sight of the picture. It was in San Jose, at the Liberty. He and Marie had been married two days, and were living in that glamorous world of the honeymoon, so poignantly sweet, so marvelous—and so fleeting. He had whispered that the girl looked like her, and she had leaned heavily against his shoulder. In the dusk of lowered lights their hands had groped and found each other, and clung.

The girl did look like Marie. When she turned her head with that little tilt of the chin, when she smiled, she was like Marie. Bud leaned forward, staring, his brows drawn together, breathing the short, quick breaths of emotion focussed upon one object, excluding all else. Once, when Frank moved his body a little in the next seat, Bud's hand went out that way involuntarily. The touch of Frank's rough coat sleeve recalled him brutally, so that he drew away with a wincing movement as though he had been hurt.

All those months in the desert; all those months of the slow journeying northward; all the fought battles with memory, when he thought that he had won—all gone for nothing, their slow anodyne serving but to sharpen now the bite of merciless remembering. His hand shook upon his knee. Small beads of moisture oozed out upon his forehead. He sat stunned before the amazing revelation of how little time and distance had done to heal his hurt.

He wanted Marie. He wanted her more than he had ever wanted her in the old days, with a tenderness, an impulse to shield her from her own weaknesses, her own mistakes. Then—in those old days—there had been the glamor of mystery that is called romance. That was gone, worn away by the close intimacies of matrimony. He knew her faults, he knew how she looked when she was angry and petulant. He knew how little the real Marie resembled the speciously amiable, altogether attractive Marie who faced a smiling world when she went pleasuring. He knew, but—he wanted her just the same. He wanted to tell her so many things about the burros, and about the desert—things that would make her laugh, and things that would make her blink back the tears. He was homesick for her as he had never been homesick in his life before. The picture flickered on through scene after scene that Bud did not see at all, though he was staring unwinkingly at the screen all the while. The love scenes at the last were poignantly real, but they passed before his eyes unnoticed. Bud's mind was dwelling upon certain love scenes of his own. He was feeling Marie's presence beside him there in the dusk.

"Poor kid—she wasn't so much to blame," he muttered just above his breath, when the screen was swept clean and blank at the end of the last reel.

"Huh? Oh, he was the big mutt, right from the start," Frank replied with the assured air of a connoisseur. "He didn't have the brains of a bluejay, or he'd have known all the time she was strong for him."

"I guess that's right," Bud mumbled, but he did not mean what Frank thought he meant. "Let's go. I want a drink."

Frank was willing enough; too willing, if the truth were known. They went out into the cool starlight, and hurried across the side street that was no more than a dusty roadway, to the saloon where they had spent the afternoon. Bud called for whisky, and helped himself twice from the bottle which the bartender placed between them. He did not speak until the second glass was emptied, and then he turned to Frank with a purple glare in his eyes.

"Let's have a game of pool or something," he suggested.

"There's a good poker game going, back there," vouchsafed the bartender, turning his thumb toward the rear, where half a dozen men were gathered in a close group around a table. "There's some real money in sight, to-night."

"All right, let's go see." Bud turned that way, Frank following like a pet dog at his heels.

At dawn the next morning, Bud got up stiffly from the chair where he had spent the night. His eyeballs showed a network of tiny red veins, swollen with the surge of alcohol in his blood and with the strain of staring all night at the cards. Beneath his eyes were puffy ridges. His cheekbones flamed with the whisky flush. He cashed in a double-handful of chips, stuffed the money he had won into his coat pocket, walked, with that stiff precision of gait by which a drunken man strives to hide his drunkenness, to the bar and had another drink. Frank was at his elbow. Frank was staggering, garrulous, laughing a great deal over very small jokes.

"I'm going to bed," said Bud, his tongue forming the words with a slow carefulness.

"Come over to my shack, Bud—rotten hotel. My bed's clean, anyway." Frank laughed and plucked him by the sleeve.

"All right," Bud consented gravely. "We'll take a bottle along."

CHAPTER TEN.
EMOTIONS ARE TRICKY THINGS

A man's mind is a tricky thing—or, speaking more exactly, a man's emotions are tricky things. Love has come rushing to the beck of a tip-tilted chin, or the tone of a voice, or the droop of an eyelid. It has fled for cause as slight. Sometimes it runs before resentment for a real or fancied wrong, but then, if you have observed it closely, you will see that quite frequently, when anger grows slow of foot, or dies of slow starvation, love steals back, all unsuspected and unbidden—and mayhap causes much distress by his return. It is like a sudden resurrection of all the loved, long-mourned dead that sleep so serenely in their tended plots. Loved though they were and long mourned, think of the consternation if they all came trooping back to take their old places in life! The old places that have been filled, most of them, by others who are loved as dearly, who would be mourned if they were taken away.

Psychologists will tell us all about the subconscious mind, the hidden loves and hates and longings which we believe are dead and long forgotten. When one of those emotions suddenly comes alive and stands, terribly real and intrusive, between our souls and our everyday lives, the strongest and the best of us may stumble and grope blindly after content, or reparation, or forgetfulness, or whatever seems most likely to give relief.

I am apologizing now for Bud, who had spent a good many months in pushing all thoughts of Marie out of his mind, all hunger for her out of his heart. He had kept away from towns, from women, lest he be reminded too keenly of his matrimonial wreck. He had stayed with Cash and had hunted gold, partly because Cash never seemed conscious of any need of a home or love or wife or children, and therefore never reminded Bud of the home and the wife and the love and the child he had lost out of his own life. Cash seldom mentioned women at all, and when he did it was in a purely general way, as women touched some other subject he was discussing. He never paid any attention to the children they met casually in their travels. He seemed absolutely self-sufficient, interested only in the prospect of finding a paying claim. What he would do with wealth, if so be he attained it, he never seemed to know or care. He never asked Bud any questions about his private affairs, never seemed to care how Bud had lived, or where. And Bud thankfully left his past behind the wall of silence. So he had come to believe that he was almost as emotion-proof as Cash appeared to be, and had let it go at that.

Now here he was, with his heart and his mind full of Marie—after more than a year and a half of forgetting her! Getting drunk and playing poker all night did not help him at all, for when he woke it was from a sweet, intimate dream of her, and it was to a tormenting desire for her, that gnawed at his mind as hunger gnaws at the stomach. Bud could not understand it. Nothing like that had ever happened to him before. By all his simple rules of reckoning he ought to be "over it" by now. He had been, until he saw that picture.

He was so very far from being over his trouble that he was under it; a beaten dog wincing under the blows of memory, stung by the lash of his longing. He groaned, and Frank thought it was the usual "morning after" headache, and laughed ruefully.

"Same here," he said. "I've got one like a barrel, and I didn't punish half the booze you did."

Bud did not say anything, but he reached for the bottle, tilted it and swallowed three times before he stopped.

"Gee!" whispered Frank, a little enviously.

Bud glanced somberly across at Frank, who was sitting by the stove with his jaws between his palms and his hair toweled, regarding his guest speculatively.

"I'm going to get drunk again," Bud announced bluntly. "If you don't want to, you'd better duck. You're too easy led—I saw that last night. You follow anybody's lead that you happen to be with. If you follow my lead to-day, you'll be petrified by night. You better git, and let me go it alone."

Frank laughed uneasily. "Aw, I guess you ain't all that fatal, Bud. Let's go over and have some breakfast—only it'll be dinner."

"You go, if you want to." Bud tilted the bottle again, his eyes half closed while he swallowed. When he had finished, he shuddered violently at the taste of the whisky. He got up, went to the water bucket and drank half a dipper of water. "Good glory! I hate whisky," he grumbled. "Takes a barrel to have any effect on me too." He turned and looked down at Frank with a morose kind of pity. "You go on and get your breakfast, kid. I don't want any. I'll stay here for awhile."

He sat down on the side of the cheap, iron bedstead, and emptied his pockets on the top quilt. He straightened the crumpled bills and counted them, and sorted the silver pieces. All told, he had sixty-three dollars and twenty cents. He sat fingering the money absently, his mind upon other things. Upon Marie and the baby, to be exact. He was fighting the impulse to send Marie the money. She might need it for the kid. If he was sure her mother wouldn't get any of it... A year and a half was quite a while, and fifteen hundred dollars wasn't much to live on these days. She couldn't work, with the baby on her hands...

Frank watched him curiously, his jaws still resting between his two palms, his eyes red-rimmed and swollen, his lips loose and trembling. A dollar alarm clock ticked resonantly, punctuated now and then by the dull clink of silver as Bud lifted a coin and let it drop on the little pile.

"Pretty good luck you had last night," Frank ventured wishfully. "They cleaned me."

Bud straightened his drooping shoulders and scooped the money into his hand. He laughed recklessly, and got up. "We'll try her another whirl, and see if luck'll bring luck. Come on—let's go hunt up some of them marks that got all the dough last night. We'll split, fifty-fifty, and the same with what we win. Huh?"

"You're on, ho—let's go." Bud had gauged him correctly—Frank would follow any one who would lead. He got up and came to the table where Bud was dividing the money into two equal sums, as nearly as he could make change. What was left over—and that was the three dollars and twenty cents—he tossed into the can of tobacco on a shelf.

"We'll let that ride—to sober up on, if we go broke," he grunted. "Come on—let's get action."

Action, of a sort, they proceeded to get. Luck brought luck of the same complexion. They won in fluctuating spells of good cards and judicious teamwork. They did not cheat, though Frank was ready if Bud had led him that way. Frank was ready for anything that Bud suggested. He drank when Bud drank, went from the first saloon to the one farther down and across the street, returned to the first with cheerful alacrity and much meaningless laughter when Bud signified a desire to change. It soothed Bud and irritated him by turns, this ready acquiescence of Frank's. He began to take a malicious delight in testing that acquiescence. He began to try whether he could not find the end of Frank's endurance in staying awake, his capacity for drink, his good nature, his credulity—he ran the scale of Frank's various qualifications, seeking always to establish a well-defined limitation somewhere.

But Frank was utterly, absolutely plastic. He laughed and drank when Bud suggested that they drink. He laughed and played whatever game Bud urged him into. He laughed and agreed with Bud when Bud made statements to test the credulity of anyman. He laughed and said, "Sure. Let's go!" when Bud pined for a change of scene.

On the third day Bud suddenly stopped in the midst of a game of pool which neither was steady enough to play, and gravely inspected the chalked end of his cue.

"That's about enough of this," he said. "We're drunk. We're so drunk we don't know a pocket from a prospect hole. I'm tired of being a hog. I'm going to go get another drink and sober up. And if you're the dog Fido you've been so far, you'll do the same." He leaned heavily upon the table, and regarded Frank with stern, bloodshot blue eyes.

Frank laughed and slid his cue the length of the table. He also leaned a bit heavily. "Sure," he said. "I'm ready, any time you are."

"Some of these days," Bud stated with drunken deliberation, "they'll take and hang you, Frank, for being such an agreeable cuss." He took Frank gravely by the arm and walked him to the bar, paid for two beers with almost his last dollar, and, still holding Frank firmly, walked him out of doors and down the street to

Frank's cabin. He pushed him inside and stood looking in upon him with a sour appraisement.

"You are the derndest fool I ever run across—but at that you're a good scout too," he informed Frank. "You sober up now, like I said. You ought to know better 'n to act the way you've been acting. I'm sure ashamed of you, Frank. Adios—I'm going to hit the trail for camp." With that he pulled the door shut and walked away, with that same circumspect exactness in his stride which marks the drunken man as surely as does a stagger.

He remembered what it was that had brought him to town—which is more than most men in his condition would have done. He went to the post office and inquired for mail, got what proved to be the assayer's report, and went on. He bought half a dozen bananas which did not remind him of that night when he had waited on the Oakland pier for the mysterious Foster, though they might have recalled the incident vividly to mind had he been sober. He had been wooing forgetfulness, and for the time being he had won.

Walking up the steep, winding trail that led to Nelson Flat cleared a little his fogged brain. He began to remember what it was that he had been fighting to forget. Marie's face floated sometimes before him, but the vision was misty and remote, like distant woodland seen through the gray film of a storm. The thought of her filled him with a vague discomfort now when his emotions were dulled by the terrific strain he had wilfully put upon brain and body. Resentment crept into the foreground again. Marie had made him suffer. Marie was to blame for this beastly fit of intoxication. He did not love Marie—he hated her. He did not want to see her, he did not want to think of her. She had done nothing for him but bring him trouble. Marie, forsooth! (Only, Bud put it in a slightly different way.)

Halfway to the flat, he met Cash walking down the slope where the trail seemed tunneled through deep green, so thick stood the young spruce. Cash was swinging his arms in that free stride of the man who has learned how to walk with the least effort. He did not halt when he saw Bud plodding slowly up the trail, but came on steadily, his keen, blue-gray eyes peering sharply from beneath his forward tilted hat brim. He came up to within ten feet of Bud, and stopped.

"Well!" He stood eyeing Bud appraisingly, much as Bud had eyed Frank a couple of hours before. "I was just starting out to see what had become of you," he added, his voice carrying the full weight of reproach that the words only hinted at.

"Well, get an eyeful, if that's what you come for. I'm here—and lookin's cheap." Bud's anger flared at the disapproval he read in Cash's eyes, his voice, the set of his lips.

But Cash did not take the challenge. "Did the report come?" he asked, as though that was the only matter worth discussing.

Bud pulled the letter sullenly from his pocket and gave it to Cash. He stood moodily waiting while Cash opened and read and returned it.

"Yeah. About what I thought—only it runs lighter in gold, with a higher percentage of copper. It'll pay to go on and see what's at bed rock. If the copper holds up to this all along, we'll be figuring on the gold to pay for getting the copper. This is copper country, Bud. Looks like we'd found us a copper mine." He turned and walked on beside Bud. "I dug in to quite a rich streak of sand while you was gone," he volunteered after a silence. "Coarse gold, as high as fifteen cents a pan. I figure we better work that while the weather's good, and run our tunnel in on this other when snow comes."

Bud turned his head and looked at Cash intently for a minute. "I've been drunker'n a fool for three days," he announced solemnly.

"Yeah. You look it," was Cash's dry retort, while he stared straight ahead, up the steep, shadowed trail.

CHAPTER ELEVEN.
THE FIRST STAGES

For a month Bud worked and forced himself to cheerfulness, and tried to forget. Sometimes it was easy enough, but there were other times when he must get away by himself and walk and walk, with his rifle over his shoulder as a mild pretense that he was hunting game. But if he brought any back camp it was because the game walked up and waited to be shot; half the time Bud did not know where he was going, much less whether there were deer within ten rods or ten miles.

During those spells of heartsickness he would sit all the evening and smoke and stare at some object which his mind failed to register. Cash would sit and watch him furtively; but Bud was too engrossed with his own misery to notice it. Then, quite unexpectedly, reaction would come and leave Bud in a peace that was more than half a torpid refusal of his mind to worry much over anything.

He worked then, and talked much with Cash, and made plans for the development of their mine. In that month they had come to call it a mine, and they had filed and recorded their claim, and had drawn up an agreement of partnership in it. They would "sit tight" and work on it through the winter, and when spring came they hoped to have something tangible upon which to raise sufficient capital to develop it properly. Or, times when they had done unusually well with their sandbank, they would talk optimistically about washing enough gold out of that claim to develop the other, and keep the title all in their own hands.

Then, one night Bud dreamed again of Marie, and awoke with an insistent craving for the oblivion of drunkenness. He got up and cooked the breakfast, washed the dishes and swept the cabin, and measured out two ounces of gold from what they had saved.

"You're keeping tabs on everything, Cash," he said shortly. "Just charge this up to me. I'm going to town."

Cash looked up at him from under a slanted eye-brow. His lips had a twist of pained disapproval.

"Yeah. I figured you was about due in town," he said resignedly.

"Aw, lay off that told-you-so stuff," Bud growled. "You never figured anything of the kind, and you know it." He pulled his heavy sweater down off a nail and put it on, scowling because the sleeves had to be pulled in place on his arms.

"Too bad you can't wait a day. I figured we'd have a clean-up to-morrow, maybe. She's been running pretty heavy—-"

"Well, go ahead and clean up, then. You can do it alone. Or wait till I get back."

Cash laughed, as a retort cutting, and not because he was amused. Bud swore and went out, slamming the door behind him.

It was exactly five days alter that when he opened it again. Cash was mixing a batch of sour-dough bread into loaves, and he did not say anything at all when Bud came in and stood beside the stove, warming his hands and glowering around the room. He merely looked up, and then went on with his bread making.

Bud was not a pretty sight. Four days and nights of trying to see how much whisky he could drink, and how long he could play poker without going to sleep or going broke, had left their mark on his face and his trembling hands. His eyes were puffy and red, and his cheeks were mottled, and his lips were fevered and had lost any sign of a humorous quirk at the corners. He looked ugly; as if he would like nothing better than an excuse to quarrel with Cash—since Cash was the only person at hand to quarrel with.

But Cash had not knocked around the world for nothing. He had seen men in that mood before, and he had no hankering for trouble which is vastly easier to start than it is to stop. He paid no attention to Bud. He made his loaves, tucked them into the pan and greased the top with bacon grease saved in a tomato can for such use. He set the pan on a shelf behind the stove, covered it with a clean flour sack, opened the stove door, and slid in two sticks.

"She's getting cold," he observed casually. "It'll be winter now before we know it."

Bud grunted, pulled an empty box toward him by the simple expedient of hooking his toes behind the corner, and sat down. He set his elbows on his thighs and buried his face in his hands. His hat dropped off his head and lay crown down beside him. He made a pathetic figure of miserable manhood, of strength mistreated. His fine, brown hair fell in heavy locks down over his fingers that rested on his forehead. Five minutes so, and he lifted his head and glanced around him apathetically. "Gee-man-ee, I've got a headache!" he muttered, dropping his forehead into his spread palms again.

Cash hesitated, derision hiding in the back of his eyes. Then he pushed the dented coffeepot forward on the stove.

"Try a cup of coffee straight," he said unemotionally, "and then lay down. You'll sleep it off in a few hours."

Bud did not look up, or make any move to show that he heard. But presently he rose and went heavily over to his bunk. "I don't want any darn coffee," he growled, and sprawled himself stomach down on the bed, with his face turned from the light.

Cash eyed him coldly, with the corner of his upper lip lifted a little. Whatever weaknesses he possessed, drinking and gambling had no place in the list. Nor had he any patience with those faults in others. Had Bud walked down drunk to Cash's camp, that evening when they first met, he might have received a little food doled out to him grudgingly, but he assuredly would not have slept in Cash's bed that night. That he tolerated drunkenness in Bud now would have been rather surprising to any one who knew Cash well. Perhaps he had a vague understanding of the deeps through which Bud was struggling, and so was constrained to hide his disapproval, hoping that the moral let-down was merely a temporary one.

He finished his strictly utilitarian household labor and went off up the flat to the sluice boxes. Bud had not moved from his first position on the bed, but he did not breathe like a sleeping man. Not at first; after an hour or so he did sleep, heavily and with queer, muddled dreams that had no sequence and left only a disturbed sense of discomfort behind then.

At noon or a little after Cash returned to the cabin, cast a sour look of contempt at the recumbent Bud, and built a fire in the old cookstove. He got his dinner, ate it, and washed his dishes with never a word to Bud, who had wakened and lay with his eyes half open, sluggishly miserable and staring dully at the rough spruce logs of the wall.

Cash put on his cap, looked at Bud and gave a snort, and went off again to his work. Bud lay still for awhile longer, staring dully at the wall. Finally he raised up, swung his feet to the floor, and sat there staring around the little cabin as though he had never before seen it.

"Huh! You'd think, the way he highbrows me, that Cash never done wrong in his life! Tin angel, him—I don't think. Next time, I'll tell a pinheaded world I'll have to bring home a quart or two, and put on a show right!"

Just what he meant by that remained rather obscure, even to Bud. He got up, shut his eyes very tight and then opened them wide to clear his vision, shook himself into his clothes and went over to the stove. Cash had not left the coffeepot on the stove but had, with malicious intent—or so Bud believed—put it away on the shelf so that what coffee remained was stone cold. Bud muttered and threw out the coffee, grounds and all—a bit of bachelor extravagance which only anger could drive him to—and made fresh coffee, and made it strong. He did not want it. He drank it for the work of physical regeneration it would do for him.

He lay down afterwards, and this time he dropped into a more nearly normal sleep, which lasted until Cash returned at dusk After that he lay with his face hidden, awake and thinking. Thinking, for the most part, of how dull and purposeless life was, and wondering why the world was made, or the people in it— since nobody was happy, and few even pretended to be. Did God really make the world, and man, just to play with—for a pastime? Then why bother about feeling ashamed for anything one did that was contrary to God's laws?

Why be puffed up with pride for keeping one or two of them unbroken—like Cash, for instance. Just because Cash never drank or played cards, what right had he to charge the whole atmosphere of the cabin with his contempt and his disapproval of Bud, who chose to do both?

On the other hand, why did he choose a spree as a relief from his particular bunch of ghosts? Trading one misery for another was all you could call it. Doing exactly the things that Marie's mother had predicted he would do, committing the very sins that Marie was always a little afraid he would commit—there must be some sort of twisted revenge in that, he thought, but for the life of him he could not quite see any real, permanent satisfaction in it—especially since Marie and her mother would never get to hear of it.

For that matter, he was not so sure that they would not get to hear. He remembered meeting, just on the first edge of his spree, one Joe De Barr, a cigar salesman whom he had known in San Jose. Joe knew Marie—in fact, Joe had paid her a little attention before Bud came into her life. Joe had been in Alpine between trains, taking orders for goods from the two saloons and the hotel. He had seen Bud drinking. Bud knew perfectly well how much Joe had seen him drinking, and he knew perfectly well that Joe was surprised to the point of amazement—and, Bud suspected, secretly gratified as well. Wherefore Bud had deliberately done what he could do to stimulate and emphasize both the surprise and the gratification. Why is it that most human beings feel a sneaking satisfaction in the downfall of another? Especially another who is, or has been at sometime, a rival in love or in business?

Bud had no delusions concerning Joe De Barr. If Joe should happen to meet Marie, he would manage somehow to let her know that Bud was going to the dogs—on the toboggan—down and out—whatever it suited Joe to declare him. It made Bud sore now to think of Joe standing so smug and so well dressed and so immaculate beside the bar, smiling and twisting the ends of his little brown mustache while he watched Bud make such a consummate fool of himself. At the time, though, Bud had taken a perverse delight in making himself appear more soddenly drunken, more boisterous and reckless than he really was.

Oh, well, what was the odds? Marie couldn't think any worse of him than she already thought. And whatever she thought, their trails had parted, and they would never cross again—not if Bud could help it. Probably Marie would say amen to that. He would like to know how she was getting along—and the baby, too. Though the baby had never seemed quite real to Bud, or as if it were a permanent member of the household. It was a leather-lunged, red-faced, squirming little mite, and in his heart of hearts Bud had not felt as though it belonged to him at all. He had never rocked it, for instance, or carried it in his arms. He had been afraid he might drop it, or squeeze it too hard, or break it somehow with his man's strength. When he thought of Marie he did not necessarily think of the baby, though sometimes he did, wondering vaguely how much it had grown, and if it still hollered for its bottle, all hours of the day and night.

Coming back to Marie and Joe—it was not at all certain that they would meet; or that Joe would mention him, even if they did. A wrecked home is always a touchy subject, so touchy that Joe had never intimated in his few remarks to Bud that there had ever been a Marie, and Bud, drunk as he had been, was still not too drunk to hold back the question that clamored to be spoken.

Whether he admitted it to himself or not, the sober Bud Moore who lay on his bunk nursing a headache and a grouch against the world was ashamed of the drunken Bud Moore who had paraded his drunkenness before the man who knew

Marie. He did not want Marie to hear what Joe might tell There was no use, he told himself miserably, in making Marie despise him as well as hate him. There was a difference. She might think him a brute, and she might accuse him of failing to be a kind and loving husband; but she could not, unless Joe told of his spree, say that she had ever heard of his carousing around. That it would be his own fault if she did hear, served only to embitter his mood.

He rolled over and glared at Cash, who had cooked his supper and was sitting down to eat it alone. Cash was looking particularly misanthropic as he bent his head to meet the upward journey of his coffee cup, and his eyes, when they lifted involuntarily with Bud's sudden movement, had still that hard look of bottled-up rancor that had impressed itself upon Bud earlier in the day.

Neither man spoke, or made any sign of friendly recognition. Bud would not have talked to any one in his present state of self-disgust, but for all that Cash's silence rankled. A moment their eyes met and held; then with shifted glances the souls of them drew apart—farther apart than they had ever been, even when they quarreled over Pete, down in Arizona.

When Cash had finished and was filing his pipe, Bud got up and reheated the coffee, and fried more bacon and potatoes, Cash having cooked just enough for himself. Cash smoked and gave no heed, and Bud retorted by eating in silence and in straightway washing his own cup, plate, knife, and fork and wiping clean the side of the table where he always sat. He did not look at Cash, but he felt morbidly that Cash was regarding him with that hateful sneer hidden under his beard. He knew that it was silly to keep that stony silence, but he kept telling himself that if Cash wanted to talk, he had a tongue, and it was not tied. Besides, Cash had registered pretty plainly his intentions and his wishes when he excluded Bud from his supper.

It was a foolish quarrel, but it was that kind of foolish quarrel which is very apt to harden into a lasting one.

CHAPTER TWELVE.
MARIE TAKES A DESPERATE CHANCE

Domestic wrecks may be a subject taboo in polite conversation, but Joe De Barr was not excessively polite, and he had, moreover, a very likely hope that Marie would yet choose to regard him with more favor than she had shown in the past. He did not chance to see her at once, but as soon as his work would permit he made it a point to meet her. He went about it with beautiful directness. He made bold to call her up on "long distance" from San Francisco, told her that he would be in San Jose that night, and invited her to a show.

Marie accepted without enthusiasm—and her listlessness was not lost over forty miles of telephone wire. Enough of it seeped to Joe's ears to make him twist his mustache quite furiously when he came out of the telephone booth. If she was still stuck on that fellow Bud, and couldn't see anybody else, it was high time she was told a few things about him. It was queer how a nice girl like Marie would hang on to some cheap guy like Bud Moore. Regular fellows didn't stand any show—unless they played what cards happened to fall their way. Joe, warned by her indifference, set himself very seriously to the problem of playing his cards to the best advantage.

He went into a flower store—disdaining the banked loveliness upon the corners—and bought Marie a dozen great, heavy-headed chrysanthemums, whose color he could not name to save his life, so called them pink and let it go at that. They were not pink, and they were not sweet—Joe held the bunch well away from his protesting olfactory nerves which were not educated to tantalizing odors—but they were more expensive than roses, and he knew that women raved over them. He expected Marie to rave over them, whether she liked them or not.

Fortified by these, groomed and perfumed and as prosperous looking as a tobacco salesman with a generous expense account may be, he went to San Jose on an early evening train that carried a parlor car in which Joe made himself comfortable. He fooled even the sophisticated porter into thinking him a millionaire, wherefore he arrived in a glow of self-esteem, which bred much optimism.

Marie was impressed—at least with his assurance and the chrysanthemums, over which she was sufficiently enthusiastic to satisfy even Joe. Since he had driven to the house in a hired automobile, he presently had the added satisfaction of handing Marie into the tonneau as though she were a queen entering the royal chariot, and of ordering the driver to take them out around the golf links, since it was still very early. Then, settling back with what purported to be a sigh of bliss, he regarded Marie sitting small and still and listless beside him. The glow of the chrysanthemums had already faded. Marie, with all the girlish prettiness she had ever possessed, and with an added charm that was very elusive and hard to analyze, seemed to have lost all of her old animation.

Joe tried the weather, and the small gossip of the film world, and a judiciously expurgated sketch of his life since he had last seen her. Marie answered him whenever his monologue required answer, but she was unresponsive, uninterested—bored. Joe twisted his mustache, eyed her aslant and took the plunge.

"I guess joy-ridin' kinda calls up old times, ay?" he began insidiously. "Maybe I shouldn't have brought you out for a ride; maybe it brings back painful memories, as the song goes."

"Oh, no," said Marie spiritlessly. "I don't see why it should."

"No? Well, that's good to hear you say so, girlie. I was kinda afraid maybe trouble had hit you hard. A sensitive, big-hearted little person like you. But if you've put it all outa your mind, why, that's where you're dead right. Personally, I was glad to see you saw where you'd made a mistake, and backed up. That takes grit and brains. Of course, we all make mistakes—you wasn't to blame—innocent little kid like you—"

"Yes," said Marie, "I guess I made a mistake, all right."

"Sure! But you seen it and backed up. And a good thing you did. Look what he'd of brought you to by now, if you'd stuck!"

Marie tilted back her head and looked up at the tall row of eucalyptus trees feathered against the stars. "What?" she asked uninterestedly.

"Well—I don't want to knock, especially a fellow that's on the toboggan already. But I know a little girl that's aw-fully lucky, and I'm honest enough to say so."

"Why?" asked Marie obligingly. "Why—in particular?"

"Why in particular?" Joe leaned toward her. "Say, you must of heard how Bud's going to the dogs. If you haven't, I don't want—"

"No, I hadn't heard," said Marie, looking up at the Big Dipper so that her profile, dainty and girlish still, was revealed like a cameo to Joe. "Is he? I love to watch the stars, don't you?"

"I love to watch a star," Joe breathed softly. "So you hadn't heard how Bud's turned out to be a regular souse? Honest, didn't you know it?"

"No, I didn't know it," said Marie boredly. "Has he?"

"Well, say! You couldn't tell it from the real thing! Believe me, Bud's some pickled bum, these days. I run across him up in the mountains, a month or so ago. Honest, I was knocked plumb silly—much as I knew about Bud that you never knew, I never thought he'd turn out quite so—" Joe paused, with a perfect imitation of distaste for his subject. "Say, this is great, out here," he murmured, tucking the robe around her with that tender protectiveness which stops just short of being proprietary. "Honest, Marie, do you like it?"

"Why, sure, I like it, Joe." Marie smiled at him in the star-light. "It's great, don't you think? I don't get out very often, any more. I'm working, you know—and evenings and Sundays baby takes up all my time."

"You working? Say, that's a darned shame! Don't Bud send you any money?"

"He left some," said Marie frankly. "But I'm keeping that for baby, when he grows up and needs it. He don't send any."

"Well, say! As long as he's in the State, you can make him dig up. For the kid's support, anyway. Why don't you get after him?"

Marie looked down over the golf links, as the car swung around the long curve at the head of the slope. "I don't know where he is," she said tonelessly. "Where did you see him, Joe?"

Joe's hesitation lasted but long enough for him to give his mustache end a twist. Marie certainly seemed to be well "over it." There could be no harm in telling.

"Well, when I saw him he was at Alpine; that's a little burg up in the edge of the mountains, on the W. P. He didn't look none too prosperous, at that. But he had money—he was playing poker and that kind of thing. And he was drunk as a boiled owl, and getting drunker just as fast as he knew how. Seemed to be kind of a stranger there; at least he didn't throw in with the bunch like a native would. But that was more than a month ago, Marie. He might not be there now. I could write up and find out for you."

Marie settled back against the cushions as though she had already dismissed the subject from her mind.

"Oh, don't bother about it, Joe. I don't suppose he's got any money, anyway. Let's forget him."

"You said it, Marie. Stacked up to me like a guy that's got just enough dough for a good big souse. He ain't hard to forget—is he, girlie?"

Marie laughed assentingly. And if she did not quite attain her old bubbling spirits during the evening, at least she sent Joe back to San Francisco feeling very well satisfied with himself. He must have been satisfied with himself. He must have been satisfied with his wooing also, because he strolled into a jewelry store the next morning and priced several rings which he judged would be perfectly suitable for engagement rings. He might have gone so far as to buy one, if he had been sure of the size and of Marie's preference in stones. Since he lacked detailed information, he decided to wait, but he intimated plainly to the clerk that he would return in a few days.

It was just as well that he did decide to wait, for when he tried again to see Marie he failed altogether. Marie had left town. Her mother, with an acrid tone of resentment, declared that she did not know any more than the man in the moon where Marie had gone, but that she "suspicioned" that some fool had told Marie where Bud was, and that Marie had gone traipsing after him. She had taken the baby along, which was another piece of foolishness which her mother would never have permitted had she been at home when Marie left.

Joe did not take the matter seriously, though he was disappointed at having made a fruitless trip to San Jose. He did not believe that Marie had done anything more than take a vacation from her mother's sharp-tongued rule, and for that he could not blame her, after having listened for fifteen minutes to the lady's monologue upon the subject of selfish, inconsiderate, ungrateful daughters. Remembering Marie's attitude toward Bud, he did not believe that she had gone hunting him.

Yet Marie had done that very thing. True, she had spent a sleepless night fighting the impulse, and a harassed day trying to make up her mind whether to write first, or whether to go and trust to the element of surprise to help plead her cause with Bud; whether to take Lovin Child with her, or leave him with her mother.

She definitely decided to write Bud a short note and ask him if he remembered having had a wife and baby, once upon a time, and if he never wished that he had them still. She wrote the letter, crying a little over it along toward the last, as women will. But it sounded cold-blooded and condemnatory. She wrote another, letting a little of her real self into the lines. But that sounded sentimental and moving-pictury, and she knew how Bud hated cheap sentimentalism.

So she tore them both up and put them in the little heating stove, and lighted a match and set them burning, and watched them until they withered down to gray ash, and then broke up the ashes and scattered them amongst the cinders. Marie, you must know, had learned a good many things, one of which was the unwisdom of whetting the curiosity of a curious woman.

After that she proceeded to pack a suit case for herself and Lovin Child, seizing the opportunity while her mother was visiting a friend in Santa Clara. Once the packing was began, Marie worked with a feverish intensity of purpose and an eagerness that was amazing, considering her usual apathy toward everything in her life as she was living it.

Everything but Lovin Child. Him she loved and gloried in. He was like Bud—so much like him that Marie could not have loved him so much if she had managed to hate Bud as she tried sometimes to hate him. Lovin Child was a husky youngster, and he already had the promise of being as tall and straight-limbed and square-shouldered as his father. Deep in his eyes there lurked always a twinkle, as though he knew a joke that would make you laugh—if only he dared tell it; a quizzical, secretly amused little twinkle, as exactly like Bud's as it was possible for a two-year-old twinkle to be. To go with the twinkle, he had a quirky little smile. And to better the smile, he had the jolliest little chuckle that ever came through a pair of baby lips.

He came trotting up to the suit case which Marie had spread wide open on the bed, stood up on his tippy toes, and peered in. The quirky smile was twitching his lips, and the look he turned toward Marie's back was full of twinkle. He reached into the suit case, clutched a clean handkerchief and blew his nose with solemn precision; put the handkerchief back all crumpled, grabbed a silk stocking and drew it around his neck, and was straining to reach his little red Brownie cap when

Marie turned and caught him up in her arms.

"No, no, Lovin Child! Baby mustn't. Marie is going to take her lovin' baby boy to find—" She glanced hastily over her shoulder to make sure there was no one to hear, buried her face in the baby's fat neck and whispered the wonder, "—to find hims daddy Bud! Does Lovin Man want to see hims daddy Bud? I bet he does want! I bet hims daddy Bud will be glad—Now you sit right still, and Marie will get him a cracker, an' then he can watch Marie pack him little shirt, and hims little bunny suit, and hims wooh-wooh, and hims 'tockins—"

It is a pity that Bud could not have seen the two of them in the next hour, wherein Marie flew to her hopeful task of packing her suit case, and Lovin Child was quite as busy pulling things out of it, and getting stepped on, and having to be comforted, and insisting upon having on his bunny suit, and then howling to go before Marie was ready. Bud would have learned enough to ease the ache in his heart—enough to humble him and fill him with an abiding reverence for a love that will live, as Marie's had lived, on bitterness and regret.

Nearly distracted under the lash of her own eagerness and the fear that her mother would return too soon and bully her into giving up her wild plan, Marie, carrying Lovin Child on one arm and lugging the suit case in the other hand, and half running, managed to catch a street car and climb aboard all out of breath and with her hat tilted over one ear. She deposited the baby on the seat beside her, fumbled for a nickel, and asked the conductor pantingly if she would be in time to catch the four-five to the city. It maddened her to watch the bored deliberation of the man as he pulled out his watch and regarded it meditatively.

"You'll catch it—if you're lucky about your transfer," he said, and rang up her fare and went off to the rear platform, just as if it were not a matter of life and death at all. Marie could have shaken him for his indifference; and as for the motorman, she was convinced that he ran as slow as he dared, just to drive her crazy. But even with these two inhuman monsters doing their best to make her miss the train, and with the street car she wanted to transfer to running off and leaving her at the very last minute, and with Lovin Child suddenly discovering that he wanted to be carried, and that he emphatically did not want her to carry the suit case at all, Marie actually reached the depot ahead of the four-five train. Much disheveled and flushed with nervousness and her exertions, she dragged Lovin Child up the steps by one arm, found a seat in the chair car and, a few minutes later, suddenly realized that she was really on her way to an unknown little town in an unknown part of the country, in quest of a man who very likely did not want to be found by her.

Two tears rolled down her cheeks, and were traced to the corners of her mouth by the fat, investigative finger of Lovin Child before Marie could find her handkerchief and wipe them away. Was any one in this world ever so utterly, absolutely miserable? She doubted it. What if she found Bud—drunk, as Joe had described him? Or, worse than that, what if she did not find him at all? She tried not to cry, but it seemed as though she must cry or scream. Fast as she wiped them away, other tears dropped over her eyelids upon her cheeks, and were given the absorbed attention of Lovin Child, who tried to catch each one with his finger. To distract him, she turned him around face to the window.

"See all the—pitty cows," she urged, her lips trembling so much that they would scarcely form the words. And when Lovin Child flattened a finger tip against the window and chuckled, and said "Ee? Ee?"—which was his way of saying see—Marie dropped her face down upon his fuzzy red "bunny" cap, hugged him close to her, and cried, from sheer, nervous reaction.

CHAPTER THIRTEEN.
CABIN FEVER IN THE WORST FORM

Bud Moore woke on a certain morning with a distinct and well-defined grouch against the world as he had found it; a grouch quite different from the sullen imp of contrariness that had possessed him lately. He did not know just what had caused the grouch, and he did not care. He did know, however, that he objected to the look of Cash's overshoes that stood pigeon-toed beside Cash's bed on the opposite side of the room, where Bud had not set his foot for three weeks and more. He disliked the audible yawn with which Cash manifested his return from the deathlike unconsciousness of sleep. He disliked the look of Cash's rough coat and sweater and cap, that hung on a nail over Cash's bunk. He disliked the thought of getting up in the cold—and more, the sure knowledge that unless he did get up, and that speedily, Cash would be dressed ahead of him, and starting a fire in the cookstove. Which meant that Cash would be the first to cook and eat his breakfast, and that the warped ethics of their dumb quarrel would demand that Bud pretend to be asleep until Cash had fried his bacon and his hotcakes and had carried them to his end of the oilcloth-covered table.

When, by certain well-known sounds, Bud was sure that Cash was eating, he could, without loss of dignity or without suspicion of making any overtures toward friendliness, get up and dress and cook his own breakfast, and eat it at his own end of the table. Bud wondered how long Cash, the old fool, would sulk like that. Not that he gave a darn—he just wondered, is all. For all he cared, Cash could go on forever cooking his own meals and living on his own side of the shack. Bud certainly would not interrupt him in acting the fool, and if Cash wanted to keep it up till spring, Cash was perfectly welcome to do so. It just showed how ornery a man could be when he was let to go. So far as he was concerned, he would just as soon as not have that dead line painted down the middle of the cabin floor.

Nor did its presence there trouble him in the least. Just this morning, however, the fact of Cash's stubbornness in keeping to his own side of the line irritated Bud. He wanted to get back at the old hound somehow—without giving in an inch in the mute deadlock. Furthermore, he was hungry, and he did not propose to lie there and starve while old Cash pottered around the stove. He'd tell the world he was going to have his own breakfast first, and if Cash didn't want to set in on the cooking, Cash could lie in bed till he was paralyzed, and be darned.

At that moment Cash pushed back the blankets that had been banked to his ears. Simultaneously, Bud swung his feet to the cold floor with a thump designed solely to inform Cash that Bud was getting up. Cash turned over with his back to the room and pulled up the blankets. Bud grinned maliciously and dressed as deliberately as the cold of the cabin would let him. To be sure, there was the disadvantage of having to start his own fire, but that disagreeable task was offset by the pleasure he would get in messing around as long as he could, cooking his breakfast. He even thought of frying potatoes and onions after he cooked his bacon. Potatoes and onions fried together have a lovely tendency to stick to the frying pan, especially if there is not too much grease, and if they are fried very slowly. Cash would have to do some washing and scraping, when it came his turn to cook. Bud knew just about how mad that would make Cash, and he dwelt upon the prospect relishfully.

Bud never wanted potatoes for his breakfast. Coffee, bacon, and hotcakes suited him perfectly. But just for meanness, because he felt mean and he wanted to act mean, he sliced the potatoes and the onions into the frying pan, and, to make his work artistically complete, he let them burn and stick to the pan, — after he had his bacon and hotcakes fried, of course!

He sat down and began to eat. And presently Cash crawled out into the warm room filled with the odor of frying onions, and dressed himself with the detached calm of the chronically sulky individual. Not once did the manner of either man betray any consciousness of the other's presence. Unless some detail of the day's work compelled them to speech, not once for more than three weeks had either seemed conscious of the other.

Cash washed his face and his hands, took the side of bacon, and cut three slices with the precision of long practice. Bud sopped his last hotcake in a pool of syrup and watched him from the corner of his eyes, without turning his head an inch toward Cash. His keenest desire, just then, was to see Cash when he tackled the frying pan.

But Cash disappointed him there. He took a pie tin off the shelf and laid his strips of bacon on it, and set it in the oven; which is a very good way of cooking breakfast bacon, as Bud well knew. Cash then took down the little square baking pan, greased from the last baking of bread, and in that he fried his hot cakes. As if that were not sufficiently exasperating, he gave absolutely no sign of being conscious of the frying pan any more than he was conscious of Bud. He did not overdo it by whistling, or even humming a tune—which would have given Bud an excuse to say something almost as mean as his mood. Abstractedness rode upon Cash's lined brow. Placid meditation shone forth from his keen old blue-gray eyes.

The bacon came from the oven juicy-crisp and curled at the edges and delicately browned. The cakes came out of the baking pan brown and thick and light. Cash sat down at his end of the table, pulled his own can of sugar and his own cup of sirup and his own square of butter toward him; poured his coffee, that he had made in a small lard pail, and began to eat his breakfast exactly as though he was alone in that cabin.

A great resentment filled Bud's soul to bursting, The old hound! Bud believed now that Cash was capable of leaving that frying pan dirty for the rest of the day!

A man like that would do anything! If it wasn't for that claim, he'd walk off and forget to come back.

Thinking of that seemed to crystallize into definite purpose what had been muddling his mind with vague impulses to let his mood find expression. He would go to Alpine that day. He would hunt up Frank and see if he couldn't jar him into showing that he had a mind of his own. Twice since that first unexpected spree, he had spent a good deal of time and gold dust and consumed a good deal of bad whisky and beer, in testing the inherent obligingness of Frank. The last attempt had been the cause of the final break between him and Cash. Cash had reminded Bud harshly that they would need that gold to develop their quartz claim, and he had further stated that he wanted no "truck" with a gambler and a drunkard, and that Bud had better straighten up if he wanted to keep friends with Cash.

Bud had retorted that Cash might as well remember that Bud had a half interest in the two claims, and that he would certainly stay with it. Meantime, he would tell the world he was his own boss, and Cash needn't think for a minute that Bud was going to ask permission for what he did or did not do. Cash needn't have any truck with him, either. It suited Bud very well to keep on his own side of the cabin, and he'd thank Cash to mind his own business and not step over the dead line.

Cash had laughed disagreeably and asked Bud what he was going to do—draw a chalk mark, maybe?

Bud, half drunk and unable to use ordinary good sense, had said yes, by thunder, he'd draw a chalk line if he wanted to, and if he did, Cash had better not step over it either, unless he wanted to be kicked back.

Wherefore the broad, black line down the middle of the floor to where the table stood. Obviously, he could not well divide the stove and the teakettle and the frying pan and coffeepot. The line stopped abruptly with a big blob of lampblack mixed with coal oil, just where necessity compelled them both to use the same floor space.

The next day Bud had been ashamed of the performance, but his shame could not override his stubbornness. The black line stared up at him accusingly. Cash, keeping scrupulously upon his own side of it, went coldly about his own affairs and never yielded so much as a glance at Bud. And Bud grew more moody and dissatisfied with himself, but he would not yield, either. Perversely he waited for Cash to apologize for what he had said about gamblers and drunkards, and tried to believe that upon Cash rested all of the blame.

Now he washed his own breakfast dishes, including the frying pan, spread the blankets smooth on his bunk, swept as much of the floor as lay upon his side of the dead line. Because the wind was in the storm quarter and the lowering clouds promised more snow, he carried in three big armfuls of wood and placed them upon his corner of the fireplace, to provide warmth when he returned. Cash would not touch that wood while Bud was gone, and Bud knew it. Cash would freeze first. But there was small chance of that, because a small, silent rivalry had grown from the quarrel; a rivalry to see which kept the best supply of wood, which swept cleanest under his bunk and up to the black line, which washed his dishes cleanest, and kept his shelf in the cupboard the tidiest. Before the fireplace in an evening Cash would put on wood, and when next it was needed, Bud would get up and put on wood. Neither would stoop to stinting or to shirking, neither would give the other an inch of ground for complaint. It was not enlivening to live together that way, but it worked well toward keeping the cabin ship shape.

So Bud, knowing that it was going to storm, and perhaps dreading a little the long monotony of being housed with a man as stubborn as himself, buttoned a coat over his gray, roughneck sweater, pulled a pair of mail-order mittens over his mail-order gloves, stamped his feet into heavy, three-buckled overshoes, and set out to tramp fifteen miles through the snow, seeking the kind of pleasure which turns to pain with the finding.

He knew that Cash, out by the woodpile, let the axe blade linger in the cut while he stared after him. He knew that Cash would be lonesome without him, whether Cash ever admitted it or not. He knew that Cash would be passively anxious until he returned—for the months they had spent together had linked them closer than either would confess. Like a married couple who bicker and nag continually when together, but are miserable when apart, close association had become a deeply grooved habit not easily thrust aside. Cabin fever might grip them and impel them to absurdities such as the dead line down the middle of their floor and the silence that neither desired but both were too stubborn to break; but it could not break the habit of being together. So Bud was perfectly aware of the fact that he would be missed, and he was ill-humored enough to be glad of it. Frank, if he met Bud that day, was likely to have his amiability tested to its limit.

Bud tramped along through the snow, wishing it was not so deep, or else deep enough to make snow-shoeing practicable in the timber; thinking too of Cash and how he hoped Cash would get his fill of silence, and of Frank, and wondering where he would find him. He had covered perhaps two miles of the fifteen, and had walked off a little of his grouch, and had stopped to unbutton his coat, when he heard the crunching of feet in the snow, just beyond a thick clump of young spruce.

Bud was not particularly cautious, nor was he averse to meeting people in the trail. He stood still though, and waited to see who was coming that way—since travelers on that trail were few enough to be noticeable.

In a minute more a fat old squaw rounded the spruce grove and shied off startled when she glimpsed Bud. Bud grunted and started on, and the squaw stepped clear of the faintly defined trail to let him pass. Moreover, she swung her shapeless body around so that she half faced him as he passed. Bud's lips tightened, and he gave her only a glance. He hated fat old squaws that were dirty and wore their hair straggling down over their crafty, black eyes. They burlesqued womanhood in a way that stirred always a smoldering resentment against them. This particular squaw had nothing to commend her to his notice. She had a dirty red bandanna tied over her dirty, matted hair and under her grimy double chin. A grimy gray blanket was draped closely over her squat shoulders and formed a pouch behind, wherein the plump form of a papoose was cradled, a little red cap pulled down over its ears.

Bud strode on, his nose lifted at the odor of stale smoke that pervaded the air as he passed. The squaw, giving him a furtive stare, turned and started on, bent under her burden.

Then quite suddenly a wholly unexpected sound pursued Bud and halted him in the trail; the high, insistent howl of a child that has been denied its dearest desire of the moment. Bud looked back inquiringly. The squaw was hurrying on, and but for the straightness of the trail just there, her fat old canvas-wrapped legs would have carried her speedily out of sight. Of course, papooses did yell once in awhile, Bud supposed, though he did not remember ever hearing one howl like that on the trail. But what made the squaw in such a deuce of a hurry all at once?

Bud's theory of her kind was simple enough: If they fled from you, it was because they had stolen something and were afraid you would catch them at it. He swung around forthwith in the trail and went after her—whereat she waddled faster through the snow like a frightened duck.

"Hey! You come back here a minute! What's all the rush?" Bud's voice and his long legs pursued, and presently he overtook her and halted her by the simple expedient of grasping her shoulder firmly. The high-keyed howling ceased as suddenly as it had begun, and Bud, peering under the rolled edge of the red stocking cap, felt his jaw go slack with surprise.

The baby was smiling at him delightedly, with a quirk of the lips and a twinkle lodged deep somewhere in its eyes. It worked one hand free of its odorous wrappings, spread four fat fingers wide apart over one eye, and chirped, "Pik-k?" and chuckled infectiously deep in its throat.

Bud gulped and stared and felt a warm rush of blood from his heart up into his head. A white baby, with eyes that laughed, and quirky red lips that laughed with the eyes, and a chuckling voice like that, riding on the back of that old squaw, struck him dumb with astonishment.

"Good glory!" he blurted, as though the words had been jolted from him by the shock. Where-upon the baby reached out its hand to him and said haltingly, as though its lips had not yet grown really familiar with the words:

"Take—Uvin—Chal!"

The squaw tried to jerk away, and Bud gave her a jerk to let her know who was boss. "Say, where'd you git that kid?" he demanded aggressively.

She moved her wrapped feet uneasily in the snow, flickered a filmy, black eyed glance at Bud's uncompromising face, and waved a dirty paw vaguely in a wide sweep that would have kept a compass needle revolving if it tried to follow and was not calculated to be particularly enlightening.

"Lo-ong ways," she crooned, and her voice was the first attractive thing Bud had discovered about her. It was pure melody, soft and pensive as the cooing of a wood dove.

"Who belongs to it?" Bud was plainly suspicious. The shake of the squaw's bandannaed head was more artfully vague than her gesture. "Don' know—modder die—fadder die—ketchum long ways—off."

"Well, what's its name?" Bud's voice harshened with his growing interest and bewilderment. The baby was again covering one twinkling eye with its spread, pink palm, and was saying "Pik-k?" and laughing with the funniest little squint to its nose that Bud had ever seen. It was so absolutely demoralizing that to relieve himself Bud gave the squaw a shake. This tickled the baby so much that the chuckle burst into a rollicking laugh, with a catch of the breath after each crescendo tone that made it absolutely individual and like none other—save one.

"What's his name?" Bud bullied the squaw, though his eyes were on the baby.

"Don't know!"

"Take—Uvin—Chal," the baby demanded imperiously.

"Uh—uh—uh? Take!"

"Uvin Chal? Now what'd yuh mean by that, oletimer?" Bud obeyed an overpowering impulse to reach out and touch the baby's cheek with a mittened thumb. The baby responded instantly by again demanding that Bud should take.

"Pik-k?" said Bud, a mitten over one eye.

"Pik-k?" said the baby, spreading his fat hand again and twinkling at Bud between his fingers. But immediately afterwards it gave a little, piteous whimper. "Take—Uvin Chal!" it beseeched Bud with voice and starlike blue eyes together. "Take!"

There was that in the baby's tone, in the unbaby-like insistence of its bright eyes, which compelled obedience. Bud had never taken a baby of that age in his arms. He was always in fear of dropping it, or crushing it with his man's strength, or something. He liked them—at a safe distance. He would chuck one under the chin, or feel diffidently the soft little cheek, but a closer familiarity scared him. Yet when this baby wriggled its other arm loose and demanded him to take, Bud reached out and grasped its plump little red-sweatered body firmly under the armpits and drew it forth, squirming with eagerness.

"Well, I'll tell the world I don't blame yuh for wanting to git outa that hog's nest," said Bud, answering the baby's gleeful chuckle.

Freed from his detaining grip on her shoulder, the squaw ducked unexpectedly and scuttled away down the trail as fast as her old legs would carry her; which was surprisingly speedy for one of her bulk. Bud had opened his mouth to ask her again where she had gotten that baby. He left it open while he stared after her astonished until the baby put up a hand over one of Bud's eyes and said "Pik-k?" with that distracting little quirk at the corners of its lips.

"You son of a gun!" grinned Bud, in the tone that turned the epithet in to a caress. "You dog gone little devil, you! Pik-k! then, if that's what you want."

The squaw had disappeared into the thick under growth, leaving a track like a hippo in the snow. Bud could have overtaken her, of course, and he could have made her take the baby back again. But he could not face the thought of it. He made no move at all toward pursuit, but instead he turned his face toward Alpine, with some vague intention of turning the baby over to the hotel woman there and getting the authorities to hunt up its parents. It was plain enough that the squaw had no right to it, else she would not have run off like that.

Bud walked at least a rod toward Alpine before he swung short around in his tracks and started the other way. "No, I'll be doggoned if I will!" he said. "You can't tell about women, no time. She might spank the kid, or something. Or maybe she wouldn't feed it enough. Anyway, it's too cold, and it's going to storm pretty pronto. Hey! Yuh cold, old-timer?"

The baby whimpered a little and snuggled its face down against Bud's chest. So Bud lifted his foot and scraped some snow off a nearby log, and set the baby down there while he took off his coat and wrapped it around him, buttoning it like a bag over arms and all. The baby watched him knowingly, its eyes round and dark blue and shining, and gave a contented little wriggle when Bud picked it up again in his arms.

"Now you're all right till we get to where it's warm," Bud assured it gravely. "And we'll do some steppin', believe me. I guess maybe you ain't any more crazy over that Injun smell on yuh, than what I am—and that ain't any at all." He walked a few steps farther before he added grimly, "It'll be some jolt for Cash, doggone his skin. He'll about bust, I reckon. But we don't give a darn. Let him bust if he wants to—half the cabin's mine, anyway."

So, talking a few of his thoughts aloud to the baby, that presently went to sleep with its face against his shoulder, Bud tramped steadily through the snow, carrying Lovin Child in his arms. No remote glimmer of the wonderful thing Fate had done for him seeped into his consciousness, but there was a new, warm glow in his heart—the warmth that came from a child's unquestioning faith in his protecting tenderness.

CHAPTER FOURTEEN.
CASH GETS A SHOCK

It happened that Cash was just returning to the cabin from the Blind Ledge claim. He met Bud almost at the doorstep, just as Bud was fumbling with the latch, trying to open the door without moving Lovin Child in his arms. Cash may or may not have been astonished. Certainly he did not betray by more than one quick glance that he was interested in Bud's return or in the mysterious burden he bore. He stepped ahead of Bud and opened the door without a word, as if he always did it just in that way, and went inside.

Bud followed him in silence, stepped across the black line to his own side of the room and laid Lovin Child carefully down so as not to waken him. He unbuttoned the coat he had wrapped around him, pulled off the concealing red cap and stared down at the pale gold, silky hair and the adorable curve of the soft cheek and the lips with the dimples tricked in at the corners; the lashes lying like the delicate strokes of an artist's pencil under the closed eyes. For at least five minutes he stood without moving, his whole face softened into a boyish wistfulness. By the stove Cash stood and stared from Bud to the sleeping baby, his bushy eyebrows lifted, his gray eyes a study of incredulous bewilderment.

Then Bud drew a long breath and seemed about to move away from the bank, and Cash turned abruptly to the stove and lifted a rusty lid and peered into the cold firebox, frowning as though he was expecting to see fire and warmth where only a sprinkle of warm ashes remained. Stubbornness held him mute and outwardly indifferent. He whittled shavings and started a fire in the cook stove, filled the teakettle and set it on to boil, got out the side of bacon and cut three slices, and never once looked toward the bunk. Bud might have brought home a winged angel, or a rainbow, or a casket of jewels, and Cash would not have permitted himself to show any human interest.

But when Bud went teetering from the cabin on his toes to bring in some pine cones they had saved for quick kindling, Cash craned his neck toward the little bundle on the bunk. He saw a fat, warm little hand stir with some baby dream. He listened and heard soft breathing that stopped just short of being an infantile snore. He made an errand to his own bunk and from there inspected the mystery at closer range. He saw a nose and a little, knobby chin and a bit of pinkish forehead with the pale yellow of hair above. He leaned and cocked his head to one side to see more—but at that moment he heard Bud stamping off the snow from his feet on the doorstep, and he took two long, noiseless strides to the dish cupboard and was fumbling there with his back to the bunk when Bud came tiptoeing in.

Bud started a fire in the fireplace and heaped the dry limbs high. Cash fried his bacon, made his tea, and set the table for his midday meal. Bud waited for the baby to wake, looking at his watch every minute or two, and making frequent cautious trips to the bunk, peeking and peering to see if the child was all right. It seemed unnatural that it should sleep so long in the daytime. No telling what that squaw had done to it; she might have doped it or something. He thought the kid's face looked red, as if it had fever, and he reached down and touched anxiously the hand that was uncovered. The hand was warm—too warm, in Bud's opinion. It would be just his luck if the kid got sick, he'd have to pack it clear in to Alpine in his arms. Fifteen miles of that did not appeal to Bud, whose arms ached after the two-mile trip with that solid little body lying at ease in the cradle they made.

His back to that end of the room, Cash sat stiff-necked and stubbornly speechless, and ate and drank as though he were alone in the cabin. Whenever Bud's mind left Lovin Child long enough to think about it, he watched Cash furtively for some sign of yielding, some softening of that grim grudge. It seemed to him as though Cash was not human, or he would show some signs of life when a live baby was brought to camp and laid down right under his nose.

Cash finished and began washing his dishes, keeping his back turned toward Bud and Bud's new possession, and trying to make it appear that he did so unconsciously. He did not fool Bud for a minute. Bud knew that Cash was nearly bursting with curiosity, and he had occasional fleeting impulses to provoke Cash to speech of some sort. Perhaps Cash knew what was in Bud's mind. At any rate he left the cabin and went out and chopped wood for an hour, furiously raining chips into the snow.

When he went in with his arms piled full of cut wood, Bud had the baby sitting on one corner of the table, and was feeding it bread and gravy as the nearest approach to baby food he could think of. During occasional interludes in the steady procession of bits of bread from the plate to the baby's mouth, Lovin Child would suck a bacon rind which he held firmly grasped in a greasy little fist. Now and then Bud would reach into his hip pocket, pull out his handkerchief as a makeshift napkin, and would carefully wipe the border of gravy from the baby's mouth, and stuff the handkerchief back into his pocket again.

Both seemed abominably happy and self-satisfied. Lovin Child kicked his heels against the rough table frame and gurgled unintelligible conversation whenever he was able to articulate sounds. Bud replied with a rambling monologue that implied a perfect understanding of Lovin Child's talk—and incidentally doled out information for Cash's benefit.

Cash cocked an eye at the two as he went by, threw the wood down on his side of the hearth, and began to replenish the fire. If he heard, he gave no sign of understanding or interest.

"I'll bet that old squaw musta half starved yah," Bud addressed the baby while he spooned gravy out of a white enamel bowl on to the second slice of bread. "You're putting away grub like a nigger at a barbecue. I'll tell the world I don't know what woulda happened if I hadn't run across yuh and made her hand yuh over."

"Ja—ja—ja—jah!" said Lovin Child, nodding his head and regarding Bud with the twinkle in his eyes.

"And that's where you're dead right, Boy. I sure do wish you'd tell me your name; but I reckon that's too much to ask of a little geezer like you. Here. Help yourself, kid—you ain't in no Injun camp now. You're with white folks now."

Cash sat down on the bench he had made for himself, and stared into the fire. His whole attitude spelled abstraction; nevertheless he missed no little sound behind him.

He knew that Bud was talking largely for his benefit, and he knew that here was the psychological time for breaking the spell of silence between them. Yet he let the minutes slip past and would not yield. The quarrel had been of Bud's making in the first place. Let Bud do the yielding, make the first step toward amity.

But Bud had other things to occupy him just then. Having eaten all his small stomach would hold, Lovin Child wanted to get down and explore. Bud had other ideas, but they did not seem to count for much with Lovin Child, who had an insistent way that was scarcely to be combated or ignored.

"But listen here, Boy!" Bud protested, after he had for the third time prevented Lovin Child from backing off the table. "I was going to take off these dirty duds and wash some of the Injun smell off yuh. I'll tell a waiting world you need a bath, and your clothes washed."

"Ugh, ugh, ugh," persisted Lovin Child, and pointed to the floor.

So Bud sighed and made a virtue of defeat. "Oh, well, they say it's bad policy to take a bath right after yuh eat. We'll let it ride awhile, but you sure have got to be scrubbed a plenty before you can crawl in with me, old-timer," he said, and set him down on the floor.

Lovin Child went immediately about the business that seemed most important. He got down on his hands and knees and gravely inspected the broad black line, hopefully testing it with tongue and with fingers to see if it would yield him anything in the way of flavor or stickiness. It did not. It had been there long enough to be thoroughly dry and tasteless. He got up, planted both feet on it and teetered back and forth, chuckling up at Bud with his eyes squinted.

He teetered so enthusiastically that he sat down unexpectedly and with much emphasis. That put him between two impulses, and while they battled he stared round-eyed at Bud. But he decided not to cry, and straightway turned himself into a growly bear and went down the line on all fours toward Cash, growling "Ooooooo!" as fearsomely as his baby throat was capable of growling.

But Cash would not be scared. He refused absolutely to jump up and back off in wild-eyed terror, crying out "Ooh! Here comes a bear!" the way Marie had always done—the way every one had always done, when Lovin Child got down and came at them growling. Cash sat rigid with his face to the fire, and would not look.

Lovin Child crawled all around him and growled his terriblest. For some unexplainable reason it did not work. Cash sat stiff as though he had turned to some insensate metal. From where he sat watching—curious to see what Cash would do—Bud saw him flinch and stiffen as a man does under pain. And because Bud had a sore spot in his own heart, Bud felt a quick stab of understanding and sympathy. Cash Markham's past could not have been a blank; more likely it held too much of sorrow for the salve of speech to lighten its hurt. There might have been a child....

"Aw, come back here!" Bud commanded Lovin Child gruffly.

But Lovin Child was too busy. He had discovered in his circling of Cash, the fanny buckles on Cash's high overshoes. He was investigating them as he had investigated the line, with fingers and with pink tongue, like a puppy. From the lowest buckle he went on to the top one, where Cash's khaki trousers were tucked inside with a deep fold on top. Lovin Child's small forefinger went sliding up in the mysterious recesses of the fold until they reached the flat surface of the knee. He looked up farther, studying Cash's set face, sitting back on his little heels while he did so. Cash tried to keep on staring into the fire, but in spite of himself his eyes lowered to meet the upward look.

"Pik-k?" chirped Lovin Child, spreading his fingers over one eye and twinkling up at Cash with the other.

Cash flinched again, wavered, swallowed twice, and got up so abruptly that Lovin Child sat down again with a plunk. Cash muttered something in his throat and rushed out into the wind and the slow-falling tiny white flakes that presaged the storm.

Until the door slammed shut Lovin Child looked after him, scowling, his eyes a blaze of resentment. He brought his palms together with a vicious slap, leaned over, and bumped his forehead deliberately and painfully upon the flat rock hearth, and set up a howl that could have been heard for three city blocks.

CHAPTER FIFTEEN.
AND BUD NEVER GUESSED

That night, when he had been given a bath in the little zinc tub they used for washing clothes, and had been carefully buttoned inside a clean undershirt of Bud's, for want of better raiment, Lovin Child missed something out of his sleepy-time cudding. He wanted Marie, and he did not know how to make his want known to this big, tender, awkward man who had befriended him and filled his thoughts till bedtime. He began to whimper and look seekingly around the little cabin. The whimper grew to a cry which Bud's rude rocking back and forth on the box before the fireplace could not still.

"M'ee—take!" wailed Lovin Child, sitting up and listening. "M'ee take—Uvin Chal!"

"Aw, now, you don't wanta go and act like that. Listen here, Boy. You lay down here and go to sleep. You can search me for what it is you're trying to say, but I guess you want your mama, maybe, or your bottle, chances are. Aw, looky!" Bud pulled his watch from his pocket—a man's infallible remedy for the weeping of infant charges—and dangled it anxiously before Lovin Child.

With some difficulty he extracted the small hands from the long limp tunnels of sleeves, and placed the watch in the eager fingers.

"Listen to the tick-tick! Aw, I wouldn't bite into it... oh, well, darn it, if nothing else'll do yuh, why, eat it up!"

Lovin Child stopped crying and condescended to take a languid interest in the watch—which had a picture of Marie pasted inside the back of the case, by the way. "Ee?" he inquired, with a pitiful little catch in his breath, and held it up for Bud to see the busy little second hand. "Ee?" he smiled tearily and tried to show Cash, sitting aloof on his bench beside the head of his bunk and staring into the fire. But Cash gave no sign that he heard or saw anything save the visions his memory was conjuring in the dancing flames.

"Lay down, now, like a good boy, and go to sleep," Bud wheedled. "You can hold it if you want to—only don't drop it on the floor—here! Quit kickin' your feet out like that! You wanta freeze? I'll tell the world straight, it's plumb cold and snaky outside to-night, and you're pretty darn lucky to be here instead of in some Injun camp where you'd have to bed down with a mess of mangy dogs, most likely. Come on, now—lay down like a good boy!"

"M'ee! M'ee take!" teased Lovin Child, and wept again; steadily, insistently, with a monotonous vigor that rasped Bud's nerves and nagged him with a vague memory of something familiar and unpleasant. He rocked his body backward and forward, and frowned while he tried to lay hold of the memory. It was the high-keyed wailing of this same man-child wanting his bottle, but it eluded Bud completely. There was a tantalizing sense of familiarity with the sound, but the lungs and the vocal chords of Lovin Child had developed amazingly in two years, and he had lost the small-infant wah-hah.

Bud did not remember, bat for all that his thoughts went back across those two years and clung to his own baby, and he wished poignantly that he knew how it was getting along; and wondered if it had grown to be as big a handful as this youngster, and how Marie would handle the emergency he was struggling with now: a lost, lonesome baby boy that would not go to sleep and could not tell why.

Yet Lovin Child was answering every one of Bud's mute questions. Lying there in his "Daddy Bud's" arms, wrapped comically in his Daddy Bud's softest undershirt, Lovin Child was proving to his Daddy Bud that his own man-child was strong and beautiful and had a keen little brain behind those twinkling blue eyes. He was telling why he cried. He wanted Marie to take him and rock him to sleep, just as she had rocked him to sleep every night of his young memory, until that time when he had toddled out of her life and into a new and peculiar world that held no Marie.

By and by he slept, still clinging to the watch that had Marie's picture in the back. When he was all limp and rosy and breathing softly against Bud's heart, Bud tiptoed over to the bunk, reached down inconveniently with one hand and turned back the blankets, and laid Lovin Child in his bed and covered him carefully. On his bench beyond the dead line Cash sat leaning forward with his elbows on his knees, and sucked at a pipe gone cold, and stared abstractedly into the fire.

Bud looked at him sitting there. For the first time since their trails had joined, he wondered what Cash was thinking about; wondered with a new kind of sympathy about Cash's lonely life, that held no ties, no warmth of love. For the first time it struck him as significant that in the two years, almost, of their constant companionship, Cash's reminiscences had stopped abruptly about fifteen years back. Beyond that he never went, save now and then when he jumped a space, to the time when he was a boy. Of what dark years lay between, Bud had never been permitted a glimpse.

"Some kid—that kid," Bud observed involuntarily, for the first time in over three weeks speaking when he was not compelled to speak to Cash. "I wish I knew where he came from. He wants his mother."

Cash stirred a little, like a sleeper only half awakened. But he did not reply, and Bud gave an impatient snort, tiptoed over and picked up the discarded clothes of Lovin Child, that held still a faint odor of wood smoke and rancid grease, and, removing his shoes that he might move silently, went to work.

He washed Lovin Child's clothes, even to the red sweater suit and the fuzzy red "bunny" cap. He rigged a line before the fireplace—on his side of the dead line, to be sure—hung the little garments upon it and sat up to watch the fire while they dried.

While he rubbed and rinsed and wrung and hung to dry, he had planned the details of taking the baby to Alpine and placing it in good hands there until its parents could be found. It was stolen, he had no doubt at all. He could picture quite plainly the agony of the parents, and common humanity imposed upon him the duty of shortening their misery as much as possible. But one day of the baby's presence he had taken, with the excuse that it needed immediate warmth and wholesome food. His conscience did not trouble him over that short delay, for he was honest enough in his intentions and convinced that he had done the right thing.

Cash had long ago undressed and gone to bed, turning his back to the warm, fire-lighted room and pulling the blankets up to his ears. He either slept or pretended to sleep, Bud did not know which. Of the baby's healthy slumber there was no doubt at all. Bud put on his overshoes and went outside after more wood, so that there would be no delay in starting the fire in the morning and having the cabin warm before the baby woke.

It was snowing fiercely, and the wind was biting cold. Already the woodpile was drifted under, so that Bud had to go back and light the lantern and hang it on a nail in the cabin wall before he could make any headway at shovelling off the heaped snow and getting at the wood beneath. He worked hard for half an hour, and carried in all the wood that had been cut. He even piled Cash's end of the hearth high with the surplus, after his own side was heaped full.

A storm like that meant that plenty of fuel would be needed to keep the cabin snug and warm, and he was thinking of the baby's comfort now, and would not be hampered by any grudge.

When he had done everything he could do that would add to the baby's comfort, he folded the little garments and laid them on a box ready for morning. Then, moving carefully, he crawled into the bed made warm by the little body. Lovin Child, half wakened by the movement, gave a little throaty chuckle, murmured "M'ee," and threw one fat arm over Bud's neck and left it there.

"Gawd," Bud whispered in a swift passion of longing, "I wish you was my own kid!" He snuggled Lovin Child close in his arms and held him there, and stared dim-eyed at the flickering shadows on the wall. What he thought, what visions filled his vigil, who can say?

CHAPTER SIXTEEN.
THE ANTIDOTE

Three days it stormed with never a break, stormed so that the men dreaded the carrying of water from the spring that became ice-rimmed but never froze over; that clogged with sodden masses of snow half melted and sent faint wisps of steam up into the chill air. Cutting wood was an ordeal, every armload an achievement. Cash did not even attempt to visit his trap line, but sat before the fire smoking or staring into the flames, or pottered about the little domestic duties that could not half fill the days.

With melted snow water, a bar of yellow soap, and one leg of an old pair of drawers, he scrubbed on his knees the floor on his side of the dead line, and tried not to notice Lovin Child. He failed only because Lovin Child refused to be ignored, but insisted upon occupying the immediate foreground and in helping—much as he had helped Marie pack her suit case one fateful afternoon not so long before.

When Lovin Child was not permitted to dabble in the pan of soapy water, he revenged himself by bringing Cash's mitten and throwing that in, and crying "Ee? Ee?" with a shameless delight because it sailed round and round until Cash turned and saw it, and threw it out.

"No, no, no!" Lovin Child admonished himself gravely, and got it and threw it back again.

Cash did not say anything. Indeed, he hid a grin under his thick, curling beard which he had grown since the first frost as a protection against cold. He picked up the mitten and laid it to dry on the slab mantel, and when he returned, Lovin Child was sitting in the pan, rocking back and forth and crooning "'Ock-a-by! 'Ock-a-by!" with the impish twinkle in his eyes.

Cash was just picking him out of the pan when Bud came in with a load of wood. Bud hastily dropped the wood, and without a word Cash handed Lovin Child across the dead line, much as he would have handed over a wet puppy. Without a word Bud took him, but the quirky smile hid at the corners of his mouth, and under Cash's beard still lurked the grin.

"No, no, no!" Lovin Child kept repeating smugly, all the while Bud was stripping off his wet clothes and chucking him into the undershirt he wore for a night-gown, and trying a man's size pair of socks on his legs.

"I should say no-no-no! You doggone little rascal, I'd rather herd a flea on a hot plate! I've a plumb good notion to hog-tie yuh for awhile. Can't trust yuh a minute nowhere. Now look what you got to wear while your clothes dry!"

"Ee? Ee?" invited Lovin Child, gleefully holding up a muffled little foot lost in the depths of Bud's sock.

"Oh, I see, all right! I'll tell the world I see you're a doggone nuisance! Now see if you can keep outa mischief till I get the wood carried in." Bud set him down on the bunk, gave him a mail-order catalogue to look at, and went out again into the storm. When he came back, Lovin Child was sitting on the hearth with the socks off, and was picking bits of charcoal from the ashes and crunching them like candy in his small, white teeth. Cash was hurrying to finish his scrubbing before the charcoal gave out, and was keeping an eye on the crunching to see that Lovin Child did not get a hot ember.

"H'yah! You young imp!" Bud shouted, stubbing his toe as he hurried forward. "Watcha think you are—a fire-eater, for gosh sake?"

Cash bent his head low—it may have been to hide a chuckle. Bud was having his hands full with the kid, and he was trying to be stern against the handicap of a growing worship of Lovin Child and all his little ways. Now Lovin Child was all over ashes, and the clean undershirt was clean no longer, after having much charcoal rubbed into its texture. Bud was not overstocked with clothes; much traveling had formed the habit of buying as he needed for immediate use. With Lovin Child held firmly under one arm, where he would be sure of him, he emptied his "war-bag" on the bunk and hunted out another shirt

Lovin Child got a bath, that time, because of the ashes he had managed to gather on his feet and his hands and his head. Bud was patient, and Lovin Child was delightedly unrepentant—until he was buttoned into another shirt of Bud's, and the socks were tied on him.

"Now, doggone yuh, I'm goin' to stake you out, or hobble yuh, or some darn thing, till I get that wood in!" he thundered, with his eyes laughing. "You want to freeze? Hey? Now you're goin' to stay right on this bunk till I get through, because I'm goin' to tie yuh on. You may holler—but you little son of a gun, you'll stay safe!"

So Bud tied him, with a necktie around his body for a belt, and a strap fastened to that and to a stout nail in the wall over the bunk. And Lovin Child, when he discovered that it was not a new game but instead a check upon his activities, threw himself on his back and held his breath until he was purple, and then screeched with rage.

I don't suppose Bud ever carried in wood so fast in his life. He might as well have taken his time, for Lovin Child was in one of his fits of temper, the kind that his grandmother invariably called his father's cussedness coming out in him. He howled for an hour and had both men nearly frantic before he suddenly stopped and began to play with the things he had scorned before to touch; the things that had made him bow his back and scream when they were offered to him hopefully.

Bud, his sleeves rolled up, his hair rumpled and the perspiration standing thick on his forehead, stood over him with his hands on his hips, the picture of perturbed helplessness.

"You doggone little devil!" he breathed, his mind torn between amusement and exasperation. "If you was my own kid, I'd spank yuh! But," he added with a little chuckle, "if you was my own kid, I'd tell the world you come by that temper honestly. Darned if I wouldn't."

Cash, sitting dejected on the side of his own bunk, lifted his head, and after that his hawklike brows, and stared from the face of Bud to the face of Lovin Child. For the first time he was struck with the resemblance between the two. The twinkle in the eyes, the quirk of the lips, the shape of the forehead and, emphasizing them all, the expression of having a secret joke, struck him with a kind of shock. If it were possible... But, even in the delirium of fever, Bud had never hinted that he had a child, or a wife even. He had firmly planted in Cash's mind the impression that his life had never held any close ties whatsoever. So, lacking the clue, Cash only wondered and did not suspect.

What most troubled Cash was the fact that he had unwittingly caused all the trouble for Lovin Child. He should not have tried to scrub the floor with the kid running loose all over the place. As a slight token of his responsibility in the matter, he watched his chance when Bud was busy at the old cookstove, and tossed a rabbit fur across to Lovin Child to play with; a risky thing to do, since he did not know what were Lovin Child's little peculiarities in the way of receiving strange gifts. But he was lucky. Lovin Child was enraptured with the soft fur and rubbed it over his baby cheeks and cooed to it and kissed it, and said "Ee? Ee?" to Cash, which was reward enough.

There was a strained moment when Bud came over and discovered what it was he was having so much fun with. Having had three days of experience by which to judge, he jumped to the conclusion that Lovin Child had been in mischief again.

"Now what yuh up to, you little scallywag?" he demanded. "How did you get hold of that? Consarn your little hide, Boy..."

"Let the kid have it," Cash muttered gruffly. "I gave it to him." He got up abruptly and went outside, and came in with wood for the cookstove, and became exceedingly busy, never once looking toward the other end of the room, where Bud was sprawled upon his back on the bunk, with Lovin Child astride his middle, having a high old time with a wonderful new game of "bronk riding."

Now and then Bud would stop bucking long enough to slap Lovin Child in the face with the soft side of the rabbit fur, and Lovin Child would squint his eyes and wrinkle his nose and laugh until he seemed likely to choke. Then Bud would cry, "Ride 'im, Boy! Ride 'im an' scratch 'im. Go get 'im, cowboy—he's your meat!" and would bounce Lovin Child till he squealed with glee.

Cash tried to ignore all that. Tried to keep his back to it. But he was human, and Bud was changed so completely in the last three days that Cash could scarcely credit his eyes and his ears. The old surly scowl was gone from Bud's face, his eyes held again the twinkle. Cash listened to the whoops, the baby laughter, the old, rodeo catch-phrases, and grinned while he fried his bacon.

Presently Bud gave a whoop, forgetting the feud in his play. "Lookit, Cash! He's ridin' straight up and whippin' as he rides! He's so-o-me bronk-fighter, buh-lieve me!"

Cash turned and looked, grinned and turned away again—but only to strip the rind off a fresh-fried slice of bacon the full width of the piece. He came down the room on his own side the dead line, and tossed the rind across to the bunk.

"Quirt him with that, Boy," he grunted, "and then you can eat it if you want."

CHAPTER SEVENTEEN.
LOVIN CHILD WRIGGLES IN

On the fourth day Bud's conscience pricked him into making a sort of apology to Cash, under the guise of speaking to Lovin Child, for still keeping the baby in camp.

"I've got a blame good notion to pack you to town to-day, Boy, and try and find out where you belong," he said, while he was feeding him oatmeal mush with sugar and canned milk. "It's pretty cold, though..." He cast a slant-eyed glance at Cash, dourly frying his own hotcakes. "We'll see what it looks like after a while. I sure have got to hunt up your folks soon as I can. Ain't I, old-timer?"

That salved his conscience a little, and freed him of the uneasy conviction that Cash believed him a kidnapper. The weather did the rest. An hour after breakfast, just when Bud was downheartedly thinking he could not much longer put off starting without betraying how hard it was going to be for him to give up the baby, the wind shifted the clouds and herded them down to the Big Mountain and held them there until they began to sift snow down upon the burdened pines.

"Gee, it's going to storm again!" Bud blustered in. "It'll be snowing like all git-out in another hour. I'll tell a cruel world I wouldn't take a dog out such weather as this. Your folks may be worrying about yuh, Boy, but they ain't going to climb my carcass for packing yuh fifteen miles in a snow-storm and letting yuh freeze, maybe. I guess the cabin's big enough to hold yuh another day—what?"

Cash lifted his eyebrows and pinched in his lips under his beard. It did not seem to occur to Bud that one of them could stay in the cabin with the baby while the other carried to Alpine the news of the baby's whereabouts and its safety. Or if it did occur to Bud, he was careful not to consider it a feasible plan. Cash wondered if Bud thought he was pulling the wool over anybody's eyes. Bud did not want to give up that kid, and he was tickled to death because the storm gave him an excuse for keeping it. Cash was cynically amused at Bud's transparency. But the kid was none of his business, and he did not intend to make any suggestions that probably would not be taken anyway. Let Bud pretend he was anxious to give up the baby, if that made him feel any better about it.

That day went merrily to the music of Lovin Child's chuckling laugh and his unintelligible chatter. Bud made the discovery that "Boy" was trying to say Lovin Child when he wanted to be taken and rocked, and declared that he would tell the world the name fit, like a saddle on a duck's back. Lovin Child discovered Cash's pipe, and was caught sucking it before the fireplace and mimicking Cash's meditative pose with a comical exactness that made Bud roar. Even Cash was betrayed into speaking a whole sentence to Bud before he remembered his grudge. Taken altogether, it was a day of fruitful pleasure in spite of the storm outside.

That night the two men sat before the fire and watched the flames and listened to the wind roaring in the pines. On his side of the dead line Bud rocked his hard-muscled, big body back and forth, cradling Lovin Child asleep in his arms. In one tender palm he nested Lovin Child's little bare feet, like two fat, white mice that slept together after a day's scampering.

Bud was thinking, as he always thought nowadays, of Marie and his own boy; yearning, tender thoughts which his clumsy man's tongue would never attempt to speak. Before, he had thought of Marie alone, without the baby; but he had learned much, these last four days. He knew now how closely a baby can creep in and cling, how they can fill the days with joy. He knew how he would miss Lovin Child when the storm cleared and he must take him away. It did not seem right or just that he should give him into the keeping of strangers—and yet he must until the parents could have him back. The black depths of their grief to-night Bud could not bring himself to contemplate. Bad enough to forecast his own desolateness when Lovin Child was no longer romping up and down the dead line, looking where he might find some mischief to get into. Bad enough to know that the cabin would again be a place of silence and gloom and futile resentments over little things, with no happy little man-child to brighten it. He crept into his bunk that night and snuggled the baby up in his arms, a miserable man with no courage left in him for the future.

But the next day it was still storming, and colder than ever. No one would expect him to take a baby out in such weather. So Bud whistled and romped with Lovin Child, and would not worry about what must happen when the storm was past.

All day Cash brooded before the fire, bundled in his mackinaw and sweater. He did not even smoke, and though he seemed to feel the cold abnormally, he did not bring in any wood except in the morning, but let Bud keep the fireplace going with his own generous supply. He did not eat any dinner, and at supper time he went to bed with all the clothes he possessed piled on top of him. By all these signs, Bud knew that Cash had a bad cold.

Bud did not think much about it at first—being of the sturdy type that makes light of a cold. But when Cash began to cough with that hoarse, racking sound that tells the tale of laboring lungs, Bud began to feel guiltily that he ought to do something about it.

He hushed Lovin Child's romping, that night, and would not let him ride a bronk at bedtime. When he was asleep, Bud laid him down and went over to the supply cupboard, which he had been obliged to rearrange with everything except tin cans placed on shelves too high for a two-year-old to reach even when he stood on his tiptoes and grunted. He hunted for the small bottle of turpentine, found it and mixed some with melted bacon grease, and went over to Cash's bunk, hesitating before he crossed the dead line, but crossing nevertheless.

Cash seemed to be asleep, but his breathing sounded harsh and unnatural, and his hand, lying uncovered on the blanket, clenched and unclenched spasmodically. Bud watched him for a minute, holding the cup of grease and turpentine in his hand.

"Say," he began constrainedly, and waited. Cash muttered something and moved his hand irritatedly, without opening his eyes. Bud tried again.

"Say, you better swab your chest with this dope. Can't monkey with a cold, such weather as this."

Cash opened his eyes, gave the log wall a startled look, and swung his glance to Bud. "Yeah—I'm all right," he croaked, and proved his statement wrong by coughing violently.

Bud set down the cup on a box, laid hold of Cash by the shoulders and forced him on his back. With movements roughly gentle he opened Cash's clothing at the throat, exposed his hairy chest, and poured on grease until it ran in a tiny rivulets. He reached in and rubbed the grease vigorously with the palm of his hand, giving particular attention to the surface over the bronchial tubes. When he was satisfied that Cash's skin could absorb no more, he turned him unceremoniously on his face and repeated his ministrations upon Cash's shoulders. Then he rolled him back, buttoned his shirts for him, and tramped heavily back to the table.

"I don't mind seeing a man play the mule when he's well," he grumbled, "but he's got a right to call it a day when he gits down sick. I ain't going to be bothered burying no corpses, in weather like this. I'll tell the world I ain't!"

He went searching on all the shelves for something more that he could give Cash. He found a box of liver pills, a bottle of Jamaica ginger, and some iodine—not an encouraging array for a man fifteen miles of untrodden snow from the nearest human habitation. He took three of the liver pills—judging them by size rather than what might be their composition—and a cup of water to Cash and commanded him to sit up and swallow them. When this was accomplished, Bud felt easier as to his conscience, though he was still anxious over the possibilities in that cough.

Twice in the night he got up to put more wood on the fire and to stand beside Cash's bed and listen to his breathing. Pneumonia, the strong man's deadly foe, was what he feared. In his cow-punching days he had seen men die of it before a doctor could be brought from the far-away town. Had he been alone with Cash, he would have fought his way to town and brought help, but with Lovin Child to care for he could not take the trail.

At daylight Cash woke him by stumbling across the floor to the water bucket. Bud arose then and swore at him for a fool and sent him back to bed, and savagely greased him again with the bacon grease and turpentine. He was cheered a little when Cash cussed back, but he did not like the sound of his voice, for all that, and so threatened mildly to brain him if he got out of bed again without wrapping a blanket or something around him.

Thoroughly awakened by this little exchange of civilities, Bud started a fire in the stove and made coffee for Cash, who drank half a cup quite meekly. He still had that tearing cough, and his voice was no more than a croak; but he seemed no worse than he had been the night before. So on the whole Bud considered the case encouraging, and ate his breakfast an hour or so earlier than usual. Then he went out and chopped wood until he heard Lovin Child chirping inside the cabin like a bug-hunting meadow lark, when he had to hurry in before Lovin Child crawled off the bunk and got into some mischief.

For a man who was wintering in what is called enforced idleness in a snow-bound cabin in the mountains, Bud Moore did not find the next few days hanging heavily on his hands. Far from it.

CHAPTER EIGHTEEN.
THEY HAVE THEIR TROUBLES

To begin with, Lovin Child got hold of Cash's tobacco can and was feeding it by small handfuls to the flames, when Bud caught him. He yelled when Bud took it away, and bumped his head on the floor and yelled again, and spatted his hands together and yelled, and threw himself on his back and kicked and yelled; while Bud towered over him and yelled expostulations and reprimands and cajolery that did not cajole.

Cash turned over with a groan, his two palms pressed against his splitting head, and hoarsely commanded the two to shut up that infernal noise. He was a sick man. He was a very sick man, and he had stood the limit.

"Shut up?" Bud shouted above the din of Lovin Child. "Ain't I trying to shut him up, for gosh sake? What d'yuh want me to do?—let him throw all the tobacco you got into the fire? Here, you young imp, quit that, before I spank you! Quick, now—we've had about enough outa you! You lay down there, Cash, and quit your croaking. You'll croak right, if you don't keep covered up. Hey, Boy! My jumpin' yellow-jackets, you'd drown a Klakon till you couldn't hear it ten feet! Cash, you old fool, you shut up, I tell yuh, or I'll come over there and shut you up! I'll tell the world—Boy! Good glory! shut up-p!"

Cash was a sick man, but he had not lost all his resourcefulness. He had stopped Lovin Child once, and thereby he had learned a little of the infantile mind. He had a coyote skin on the foot of his bed, and he raised himself up and reached for it as one reaches for a fire extinguisher. Like a fire extinguisher he aimed it, straight in the middle of the uproar.

Lovin Child, thumping head and heels regularly on the floor and punctuating the thumps with screeches, was extinguished—suddenly, completely silenced by the muffling fur that fell from the sky, so far as he knew. The skin covered him completely. Not a sound came from under it. The stillness was so absolute that Bud was scared, and so was Cash, a little. It was as though Lovin Child, of a demon one instant, was in the next instant snuffed out of existence.

"What yuh done?" Bud ejaculated, rolling wild eyes at Cash. "You—"

The coyote skin rattled a little. A fluff of yellow, a spark of blue, and "Pik-k?" chirped Lovin Child from under the edge, and ducked back again out of sight.

Bud sat down weakly on a box and shook his head slowly from one side to the other. "You've got me going south," he made solemn confession to the wobbling skin—or to what it concealed. "I throw up my hands, I'll tell the world fair." He got up and went over and sat down on his bunk, and rested his hands on his knees, and considered the problem of Lovin Child.

"Here I've got wood to cut and water to bring and grub to cook, and I can't do none of them because I've got to ride herd on you every minute. You've got my goat, kid, and that's the truth. You sure have. Yes, 'Pik-k,' doggone yuh—after me going crazy with yuh, just about, and thinking you're about to blow your radiator cap plumb up through the roof! I'll tell yuh right here and now, this storm has got to let up pretty quick so I can pack you outa here, or else I've got to pen you up somehow, so I can do something besides watch you. Look at the way you scattered them beans, over there by the cupboard! By rights I oughta stand over yuh and make yuh pick every one of 'em up! and who was it drug all the ashes outa the stove, I'd like to know?"

The coyote skin lifted a little and moved off toward the fireplace, growling "Ooo-ooo-ooo!" like a bear—almost. Bud rescued the bear a scant two feet from the flames, and carried fur, baby and all, to the bunk. "My good lord, what's a fellow going to do with yuh?" he groaned in desperation. "Burn yourself up, you would! I can see now why folks keep their kids corralled in high chairs and gocarts all the time. They got to, or they wouldn't have no kids."

Bud certainly was learning a few things that he had come near to skipping altogether in his curriculum of life. Speaking of high chairs, whereof he had thought little enough in his active life, set him seriously to considering ways and means. Weinstock-Lubin had high chairs listed in their catalogue. Very nice high chairs, for one of which Bud would have paid its weight in gold dust (if one may believe his word) if it could have been set down in that cabin at that particular moment. He studied the small cuts of the chairs, holding Lovin Child off the page by main strength the while. Wishing one out of the catalogue and into the room being impracticable, he went after the essential features, thinking to make one that would answer the purpose.

Accustomed as he was to exercising his inventive faculty in overcoming certain obstacles raised by the wilderness in the path of comfort, Bud went to work with what tools he had, and with the material closest to his hand. Crude tools they were, and crude materials—like using a Stilson wrench to adjust a carburetor, he told Lovin Child who tagged him up and down the cabin. An axe, a big jack-knife, a hammer and some nails left over from building their sluice boxes, these were the tools. He took the axe first, and having tied Lovin Child to the leg of his bunk for safety's sake, he went out and cut down four young oaks behind the cabin, lopped off the branches and brought them in for chair legs. He emptied a dynamite box of odds and ends, scrubbed it out and left it to dry while he mounted the four legs, with braces of the green oak and a skeleton frame on top. Then he knocked one end out of the box, padded the edges of the box with burlap, and set Lovin Child in his new high chair.

He was tempted to call Cash's attention to his handiwork, but Cash was too sick to be disturbed, even if the atmosphere between them had been clear enough for easy converse. So he stifled the impulse and addressed himself to Lovin Child, which did just as well.

Things went better after that. Bud could tie the baby in the chair, give him a tin cup and a spoon and a bacon rind, and go out to the woodpile feeling reasonably certain that the house would not be set afire during his absence. He could cook a meal in peace, without fear of stepping on the baby. And Cash could lie as close as he liked to the edge of the bed without running the risk of having his eyes jabbed with Lovin Child's finger, or something slapped unexpectedly in his face.

He needed protection from slight discomforts while he lay there eaten with fever, hovering so close to pneumonia that Bud believed he really had it and watched over him nights as well as daytimes. The care he gave Cash was not, perhaps, such as the medical profession would have endorsed, but it was faithful and it made for comfort and so aided Nature more than it hindered.

Fair weather came, and days of melting snow. But they served only to increase Bud's activities at the woodpile and in hunting small game close by, while Lovin Child took his nap and Cash was drowsing. Sometimes he would bundle the baby in an extra sweater and take him outside and let him wallow in the snow while Bud cut wood and piled it on the sheltered side of the cabin wall, a reserve supply to draw on in an emergency.

It may have been the wet snow—more likely it was the cabin air filled with germs of cold. Whatever it was, Lovin Child caught cold and coughed croupy all one night, and fretted and would not sleep. Bud anointed him as he had anointed Cash, and rocked him in front of the fire, and met the morning hollow-eyed and haggard. A great fear tore at his heart. Cash read it in his eyes, in the tones of his voice when he crooned soothing fragments of old range songs to the baby, and at daylight Cash managed to dress himself and help; though what assistance he could possibly give was not all clear to him, until he saw Bud's glance rove anxiously toward the cook-stove.

"Hand the kid over here," Cash said huskily. "I can hold him while you get yourself some breakfast."

Bud looked at him stupidly, hesitated, looked down at the flushed little face, and carefully laid him in Cash's outstretched arms. He got up stiffly—he had been sitting there a long time, while the baby slept uneasily—and went on his tiptoes to make a fire in the stove.

He did not wonder at Cash's sudden interest, his abrupt change from moody aloofness to his old partnership in trouble as well as in good fortune. He knew that Cash was not fit for the task, however, and he hurried the coffee to the boiling point that he might the sooner send Cash back to bed. He gulped down a cup of coffee scalding hot, ate a few mouthfuls of bacon and bread, and brought a cup back to Cash.

"What d'yuh think about him?" he whispered, setting the coffee down on a box so that he could take Lovin Child. "Pretty sick kid, don't yuh think?"

"It's the same cold I got," Cash breathed huskily. "Swallows like it's his throat, mostly. What you doing for him?"

"Bacon grease and turpentine," Bud answered him despondently. "I'll have to commence on something else, though—turpentine's played out I used it most all up on you."

"Coal oil's good. And fry up a mess of onions and make a poultice." He put up a shaking hand before his mouth and coughed behind it, stifling the sound all he could.

Lovin Child threw up his hands and whimpered, and Bud went over to him anxiously. "His little hands are awful hot," he muttered. "He's been that way all night."

Cash did not answer. There did not seem anything to say that would do any good. He drank his coffee and eyed the two, lifting his eyebrows now and then at some new thought.

"Looks like you, Bud," he croaked suddenly. "Eyes, expression, mouth—you could pass him off as your own kid, if you wanted to."

"I might, at that," Bud whispered absently. "I've been seeing you in him, though, all along. He lifts his eyebrows same way you do."

"Ain't like me," Cash denied weakly, studying Lovin Child. "Give him here again, and you go fry them onions. I would—if I had the strength to get around."

"Well, you ain't got the strength. You go back to bed, and I'll lay him in with yuh. I guess he'll lay quiet. He likes to be cuddled up close."

In this way was the feud forgotten. Save for the strange habits imposed by sickness and the care of a baby, they dropped back into their old routine, their old relationship. They walked over the dead line heedlessly, forgetting why it came to be there. Cabin fever no longer tormented them with its magnifying of little things. They had no time or thought for trifles; a bigger matter than their own petty prejudices concerned them. They were fighting side by side, with the Old Man of the Scythe—the Old Man who spares not.

Lovin Child was pulling farther and farther away from them. They knew it, they felt it in his hot little hands, they read it in his fever-bright eyes. But never once did they admit it, even to themselves. They dared not weaken their efforts with any admissions of a possible defeat. They just watched, and fought the fever as best they could, and waited, and kept hope alive with fresh efforts.

Cash was tottery weak from his own illness, and he could not speak above a whisper. Yet he directed, and helped soothe the baby with baths and slow strokings of his hot forehead, and watched him while Bud did the work, and worried because he could not do more.

They did not know when Lovin Child took a turn for the better, except that they realized the fever was broken. But his listlessness, the unnatural drooping of his whole body, scared them worse than before. Night and day one or the other watched over him, trying to anticipate every need, every vagrant whim. When he began to grow exacting, they were still worried, though they were too fagged to abase themselves before him as much as they would have liked.

Then Bud was seized with an attack of the grippe before Lovin Child had passed the stage of wanting to be held every waking minute. Which burdened Cash with extra duties long before he was fit.

Christmas came, and they did not know it until the day was half gone, when Cash happened to remember. He went out then and groped in the snow and found a little spruce, hacked it off close to the drift and brought it in, all loaded with frozen snow, to dry before the fire. The kid, he declared, should have a Christmas tree, anyway. He tied a candle to the top, and a rabbit skin to the bottom, and prunes to the tip of the branches, and tried to rouse a little enthusiasm in Lovin Child. But Lovin Child was not interested in the makeshift. He was crying because Bud had told him to keep out of the ashes, and he would not look.

So Cash untied the candle and the fur and the prunes, threw them across the room, and peevishly stuck the tree in the fireplace.

"Remember what you said about the Fourth of July down in Arizona, Bud?" he asked glumly. "Well, this is the same kind of Christmas." Bud merely grunted.

CHAPTER NINETEEN.
BUD FACES FACTS

New Year came and passed and won nothing in the way of celebration from the three in Nelson's cabin. Bud's bones ached, his head ached, the flesh on his body ached. He could take no comfort anywhere, under any circumstances. He craved clean white beds and soft-footed attendance and soothing silence and cool drinks—and he could have none of those things. His bedclothes were heavy upon his aching limbs; he had to wait upon his own wants; the fretful crying of Lovin Child or the racking cough of Cash was always in his ears, and as for cool drinks, there was ice water in plenty, to be sure, but nothing else. Fair weather came, and storms, and cold: more storms and cold than fair weather. Neither man ever mentioned taking Lovin Child to Alpine. At first, because it was out of the question; after that, because they did not want to mention it. They frequently declared that Lovin Child was a pest, and there were times when Bud spoke darkly of spankings—which did not materialize. But though they did not mention it, they knew that Lovin Child was something more; something endearing, something humanizing, something they needed to keep them immune from cabin fever.

Some time in February it was that Cash fashioned a crude pair of snowshoes and went to town, returning the next day. He came home loaded with little luxuries for Lovin Child, and with the simpler medicines for other emergencies which they might have to meet, but he did not bring any word of seeking parents. The nearest he came to mentioning the subject was after supper, when the baby was asleep and Bud trying to cut a small pair of overalls from a large piece of blue duck that Cash had brought. The shears were dull, and Lovin Child's little rompers were so patched and shapeless that they were not much of a guide, so Bud was swearing softly while he worked.

"I didn't hear a word said about that kid being lost," Cash volunteered, after he had smoked and watched Bud awhile. "Couldn't have been any one around Alpine, or I'd have heard something about it."

Bud frowned, though it may have been over his tailoring problem.

"Can't tell—the old squaw mighta been telling the truth," he said reluctantly. "I s'pose they do, once in awhile. She said his folks were dead." And he added defiantly, with a quick glance at Cash, "Far as I'm concerned, I'm willing to let it ride that way. The kid's doing all right."

"Yeah. I got some stuff for that rash on his chest. I wouldn't wonder if we been feeding him too heavy on bacon rinds, Bud. They say too much of that kinda thing is bad for kids. Still, he seems to feel all right."

"I'll tell the world he does! He got hold of your old pipe to-day and was suckin' away on it, I don't know how long. Never feazed him, either. If he can stand that, I guess he ain't very delicate."

"Yeah. I laid that pipe aside myself because it was getting so dang strong. Ain't you getting them pants too long in the seat, Bud? They look to me big enough for a ten-year-old."

"I guess you don't realize how that kid's growing!" Bud defended his handiwork "And time I get the seams sewed, and the side lapped over for buttons—"

"Yeah. Where you going to get the buttons? You never sent for any."

"Oh, I'll find buttons. You can donate a couple off some of your clothes, if you want to right bad."

"Who? Me? I ain't got enough now to keep the wind out," Cash protested. "Lemme tell yuh something, Bud. If you cut more saving, you'd have enough cloth there for two pair of pants. You don't need to cut the legs so long as all that. They'll drag on the ground so the poor kid can't walk in 'em without falling all over himself."

"Well, good glory! Who's making these pants? Me, or you?" Bud exploded. "If you think you can do any better job than what I'm doing, go get yourself some cloth and fly at it! Don't think you can come hornin' in on my job, 'cause I'll tell the world right out loud, you can't."

"Yeah—that's right! Go to bellerin' around like a bull buffalo, and wake the kid up! I don't give a cuss how you make'm. Go ahead and have the seat of his pants hangin' down below his knees if you want to!" Cash got up and moved huffily over to the fireplace and sat with his back to Bud.

"Maybe I will, at that," Bud retorted. "You can't come around and grab the job I'm doing." Bud was jabbing a needle eye toward the end of a thread too coarse for it, and it did not improve his temper to have the thread refuse to pass through the eye.

Neither did it please him to find, when all the seams were sewn, that the little overalls failed to look like any garment he had ever seen on a child. When he tried them on Lovin Child, next day, Cash took one look and bolted from the cabin with his hand over his mouth.

When he came back an hour or so later, Lovin Child was wearing his ragged rompers, and Bud was bent over a Weinstock-Lubin mail-order catalogue. He had a sheet of paper half filled with items, and was licking his pencil and looking for more. He looked up and grinned a little, and asked Cash when he was going to town again; and added that he wanted to mail a letter.

"Yeah. Well, the trail's just as good now as it was when I took it," Cash hinted strongly. "When I go to town again, it'll be because I've got to go. And far as I can see, I won't have to go for quite some time."

So Bud rose before daylight the next morning, tied on the makeshift snow-shoes Cash had contrived, and made the fifteen-mile trip to Alpine and back before dark. He brought candy for Lovin Child, tended that young gentleman through a siege of indigestion because of the indulgence, and waited impatiently until he was fairly certain that the wardrobe he had ordered had arrived at the post-office. When he had counted off the two days required for a round trip to Sacramento, and had added three days for possible delay in filling the order, he went again, and returned in one of the worst storms of the winter.

But he did not grudge the hardship, for he carried on his back a bulky bundle of clothes for Lovin Child; enough to last the winter through, and some to spare; a woman would have laughed at some of the things he chose: impractical, dainty garments that Bud could not launder properly to save his life. But there were little really truly overalls, in which Lovin Child promptly developed a strut that delighted the men and earned him the title of Old Prospector. And there were little shirts and stockings and nightgowns and a pair of shoes, and a toy or two that failed to interest him at all, after the first inspection.

It began to look as though Bud had deliberately resolved upon carrying a guilty conscience all the rest of his life. He had made absolutely no effort to trace the parents of Lovin Child when he was in town. On the contrary he had avoided all casual conversation, for fear some one might mention the fact that a child had been lost. He had been careful not to buy anything in the town that would lead one to suspect that he had a child concealed upon his premises, and he had even furnished what he called an alibi when he bought the candy, professing to own an inordinately sweet tooth.

Cash cast his eyes over the stock of baby clothes which Bud gleefully unwrapped on his bunk, and pinched out a smile under his beard.

"Well, if the kid stays till he wears out all them clothes, we'll just about have to give him a share in the company," he said drily.

Bud looked up in quick jealousy. "What's mine's his, and I own a half interest in both claims. I guess that'll feed him—if they pan out anything," he retorted. "Come here, Boy, and let's try this suit on. Looks pretty small to me—marked three year, but I reckon they don't grow 'em as husky as you, back where they make all these clothes."

"Yeah. But you ought to put it in writing, Bud. S'pose anything happened to us both—and it might. Mining's always got its risky side, even cutting out sickness, which we've had a big sample of right this winter. Well, the kid oughta have some security in case anything did happen. Now—"

Bud looked thoughtfully down at the fuzzy yellow head that did not come much above his knee.

"Well, how yuh going to do anything like that without giving it away that we've got him? Besides, what name'd we give him in the company? No, sir, Cash, he gets what I've got, and I'll smash any damn man that tries to get it away from him. But we can't get out any legal papers—"

"Yeah. But we can make our wills, can't we? And I don't know where you get the idea, Bud, that you've got the whole say about him. We're pardners, ain't we? Share and share alike. Mines, mules, grub—kids—equal shares goes."

"That's where you're dead wrong. Mines and mules and grub is all right, but when it comes to this old Lovin Man, why—who was it found him, for gosh sake?"

"Aw, git out!" Cash growled. "Don't you reckon I'd have grabbed him off that squaw as quick as you did? I've humored you along, Bud, and let you hog him nights, and feed him and wash his clothes, and I ain't kicked none, have I? But when it comes to prope'ty—"

"You ain't goin' to horn in there, neither. Anyway, we ain't got so darn much the kid'll miss your share, Cash."

"Yeah. All the more reason why he'll need it I don't see how you're going to stop me from willing my share where I please. And when you come down to facts, Bud, why—you want to recollect that I plumb forgot to report that kid, when I was in town. And I ain't a doubt in the world but what his folks would be glad enough—"

"Forget that stuff!" Bud's tone was so sharp that Lovin Child turned clear around to look up curiously into his face. "You know why you never reported him, doggone yuh! You couldn't give him up no easier than I could. And I'll tell the world to its face that if anybody gets this kid now they've pretty near got to fight for him. It ain't right, and it ain't honest. It's stealing to keep him, and I never stole a brass tack in my life before. But he's mine as long as I live and can hang on to him. And that's where I stand. I ain't hidin' behind no kind of alibi. The old squaw did tell me his folks was dead; but if you'd ask me, I'd say she was lying when she said it. Chances are she stole him. I'm sorry for his folks, supposing he's got any. But I ain't sorry enough for 'em to give him up if I can help it. I hope they've got more, and I hope they've gentled down by this time and are used to being without him. Anyway, they can do without him now easier than what I can, because..." Bud did not finish that sentence, except by picking Lovin Child up in his arms and squeezing him as hard as he dared. He laid his face down for a minute on Lovin Child's head, and when he raised it his lashes were wet.

"Say, old-timer, you need a hair cut. Yuh know it?" he said, with a huskiness in his voice, and pulled a tangle playfully. Then his eyes swung round defiantly to Cash. "It's stealing to keep him, but I can't help it. I'd rather die right here in my tracks than give up this little ole kid. And you can take that as it lays, because I mean it."

Cash sat quiet for a minute or two, staring down at the floor. "Yeah. I guess there's two of us in that fix," he observed in his dry way, lifting his eyebrows while he studied a broken place in the side of his overshoe. "All the more reason why we should protect the kid, ain't it? My idea is that we ought to both of us make our wills right here and now. Each of us to name the other for guardeen, in case of accident, and each one picking a name for the kid, and giving him our share in the claims and anything else we may happen to own." He stopped abruptly, his jaw sagging a little at some unpleasant thought.

"I don't know—come to think of it, I can't just leave the kid all my property. I—I've got a kid of my own, and if she's alive—I ain't heard anything of her for fifteen years and more, but if she's alive she'd come in for a share. She's a woman grown by this time. Her mother died when she was a baby. I married the woman I hired to take care of her and the house—like a fool. When we parted, she took the kid with her. She did think a lot of her, I'll say that much for her, and that's all I can say in her favor. I drifted around and lost track of 'em. Old woman, she married again, and I heard that didn't pan out, neither. Anyway, she kept the girl, and gave her the care and schooling that I couldn't give. I was a drifter.

"Well, she can bust the will if I leave her out, yuh see. And if the old woman gets a finger in the pie, it'll be busted, all right. I can write her down for a hundred dollars perviding she don't contest. That'll fix it. And the rest goes to the kid here. But I want him to have the use of my name, understand. Something-or-other Markham Moore ought to suit all hands well enough."

Bud, holding Lovin Child on his knees, frowned a little at first. But when he looked at Cash, and caught the wistfulness in his eyes, he surrendered warm-heartedly.

"A couple of old he-hens like us—we need a chick to look after," he said whimsically. "I guess Markham Moore ought to be good enough for most any kid. And if it ain't, by gosh, we'll make it good enough! If I ain't been all I should be, there's no law against straightening up. Markham Moore goes as it lays—hey, Lovins?" But Lovin Child had gone to sleep over his foster fathers' disposal of his future. His little yellow head was wabbling on his limp neck, and Bud cradled him in his arms and held him so.

"Yeah. But what are we going to call him?" Methodical Cash wanted the whole matter settled at one conference, it seemed.

"Call him? Why, what've we been calling him, the last two months?"

"That," Cash retorted, "depended on what devilment he was into when we called!"

"You said it all, that time. I guess, come to think of it—tell you what, Cash, let's call him what the kid calls himself. That's fair enough. He's got some say in the matter, and if he's satisfied with Lovin, we oughta be. Lovin Markam Moore ain't half bad. Then if he wants to change it when he grows up, he can."

"Yeah. I guess that's as good as anything. I'd hate to see him named Cassius. Well, now's as good a time as any to make them wills, Bud. We oughta have a couple of witnesses, but we can act for each other, and I guess it'll pass. You lay the kid down, and we'll write 'em and have it done with and off our minds. I dunno—I've got a couple of lots in Phoenix I'll leave to the girl. By rights she should have 'em. Lovins, here, 'll have my share in all mining claims; these two I'll name 'specially, because I expect them to develop into paying mines; the Blind Lodge, anyway."

A twinge of jealousy seized Bud. Cash was going ahead a little too confidently in his plans for the kid. He did not want to hurt old Cash's feelings, and of course he needed Cash's assistance if he kept Lovin Child for his own. But Cash needn't think he was going to claim the kid himself.

"All right—put it that way. Only, when you're writing it down, you make it read 'child of Bud Moore' or something like that. You can will him the moon, if you want, and you can have your name sandwiched in between his and mine. But get this, and get it right. He's mine, and if we ever split up, the kid goes with me. I'll tell the world right now that this kid belongs to me, and where I go he goes. You got that?"

"You don't have to beller at the top of your voice, do yuh?" snapped Cash, prying the cork out of the ink bottle with his jackknife. "Here's another pen point. Tie it onto a stick or something and git to work before you git to putting it off."

Leaning over the table facing each other, they wrote steadily for a few minutes. Then Bud began to flag, and finally he stopped and crumpled the sheet of tablet paper into a ball. Cash looked up, lifted his eyebrows irritatedly, and went on with his composition.

Bud sat nibbling the end of his makeshift penholder. The obstacle that had loomed in Cash's way and had constrained him to reveal the closed pages of his life, loomed large in Bud's way also. Lovin Child was a near and a very dear factor in his life—but when it came to sitting down calmly and setting his affairs in order for those who might be left behind, Lovin Child was not the only person he must think of. What of his own man-child? What of Marie?

He looked across at Cash writing steadily in his precise way, duly bequeathing his worldly goods to Lovin; owning, too, his responsibilities in another direction, but still making Lovin Child his chief heir so far as he knew. On the spur of the moment Bud had thought to do the same thing. But could he do it?

He seemed to see his own baby standing wistfully aloof, pushed out of his life that this baby he had no right to keep might have all of his affections, all of his poor estate. And Marie, whose face was always in the back of his memory, a tearful, accusing vision that would not let him be—he saw Marie working in some office, earning the money to feed and clothe their child. And Lovin Child romping up and down the cabin, cuddled and scolded and cared for as best an awkward man may care for a baby—a small, innocent usurper.

Bud dropped his face in his palms and tried to think the thing out coldly, clearly, as Cash had stated his own case. Cash did not know where his own child was, and he did not seem to care greatly. He was glad to salve his conscience with a small bequest, keeping the bulk—if so tenuous a thing as Cash's fortune may be said to have bulk—for this baby they two were hiding away from its lawful parents. Cash could do it; why couldn't be? He raised his head and looked over at Lovin Child, asleep in his new and rumpled little finery. Why did his own baby come between them now, and withhold his hand from doing the same?

Cash finished, glanced curiously across at Bud, looked down at what he had written, and slid the sheet of paper across.

"You sign it, and then if you don't know just how to word yours, you can use this for a pattern. I've read law books enough to know this will get by, all right. It's plain, and it tells what I want, and that's sufficient to hold in court."

Bud read it over apathetically, signed his name as witness, and pushed the paper back.

"That's all right for you," he said heavily. "Your kid is grown up now, and besides, you've got other property to give her. But—it's different with me. I want this baby, and I can't do without him. But I can't give him my share in the claims, Cash. I—there's others that's got to be thought of first."

CHAPTER TWENTY.

LOVIN CHILD STRIKES IT RICH

It was only the next day that Bud was the means of helping Lovin Child find a fortune for himself; which eased Bud's mind considerably, and balanced better his half of the responsibility. Cutting out the dramatic frills, then, this is what happened to Lovin Child and Bud:

They were romping around the cabin, like two puppies that had a surplus of energy to work off. Part of the time Lovin Child was a bear, chasing Bud up and down the dead line, which was getting pretty well worn out in places. After that, Bud was a bear and chased Lovin. And when Lovin Child got so tickled he was perfectly helpless in the corner where he had sought refuge, Bud caught him and swung him up to his shoulder and let him grab handfuls of dirt out of the roof.

Lovin Child liked that better than being a bear, and sifted Bud's hair full of dried mud, and threw the rest on the floor, and frequently cried "Tell a worl'!" which he had learned from Bud and could say with the uncanny pertinency of a parrot.

He had signified a desire to have Bud carry him along the wall, where some lovely lumps of dirt protruded temptingly over a bulging log. Then he leaned and grabbed with his two fat hands at a particularly big, hard lump. It came away in his hands and fell plump on the blankets of the bunk, half blinding Bud with the dust that came with it.

"Hey! You'll have all the chinkin' out of the dang shack, if you let him keep that lick up, Bud," Cash grumbled, lifting his eyebrows at the mess.

"Tell a worl'!" Lovin Child retorted over his shoulder, and made another grab.

This time the thing he held resisted his baby strength. He pulled and he grunted, he kicked Bud in the chest and grabbed again. Bud was patient, and let him fuss—though in self-defense he kept his head down and his eyes away from the expected dust bath.

"Stay with it, Boy; pull the darn roof down, if yuh want. Cash'll get out and chink 'er up again."

"Yeah. Cash will not," the disapproving one amended the statement gruffly. "He's trying to get the log outa the wall, Bud."

"Well, let him try, doggone it. Shows he's a stayer. I wouldn't have any use for him if he didn't have gumption enough to tackle things too big for him, and you wouldn't either. Stay with 'er, Lovins! Doggone it, can't yuh git that log outa there nohow? Uh-h! A big old grunt and a big old heave—uh-h! I'll tell the world in words uh one syllable, he's some stayer."

"Tell a worl'!" chuckled Lovin Child, and pulled harder at the thing he wanted.

"Hey! The kid's got hold of a piece of gunny sack or something. You look out, Bud, or he'll have all that chinkin' out. There's no sense in lettin' him tear the whole blame shack to pieces, is there?"

"Can if he wants to. It's his shack as much as it's anybody's." Bud shifted Lovin Child more comfortably on his shoulder and looked up, squinting his eyes half shut for fear of dirt in them.

"For the love of Mike, kid, what's that you've got? Looks to me like a piece of buckskin, Cash. Here, you set down a minute, and let Bud take a peek up there."

"Bud—pik-k?" chirped Lovin Child from the blankets, where Bud had deposited him unceremoniously.

"Yes, Bud pik-k." Bud stepped up on the bunk, which brought his head above the low eaves. He leaned and looked, and scraped away the caked mud. "Good glory! The kid's found a cache of some kind, sure as you live!" And he began to claw out what had been hidden behind the mud.

First a buckskin bag, heavy and grimed and knobby. Gold inside it, he knew without looking. He dropped it down on the bunk, carefully so as not to smash a toe off the baby. After that he pulled out four baking-powder cans, all heavy as lead. He laid his cheek against the log and peered down the length of it, and jumped down beside the bunk.

"Kid's found a gold mine of his own, and I'll bet on it," he cried excitedly. "Looky, Cash!"

Cash was already looking, his eyebrows arched high to match his astonishment. "Yeah. It's gold, all right. Old man Nelson's hoard, I wouldn't wonder. I've always thought it was funny he never found any gold in this flat, long as he lived here. And traces of washing here and there, too. Well!"

"Looky, Boy!" Bud had the top off a can, and took out a couple of nuggets the size of a cooked Lima bean. "Here's the real stuff for yuh.

"It's yours, too—unless—did old Nelson leave any folks, Cash, do yuh know?"

"They say not. The county buried him, they say. And nobody ever turned up to claim him or what little he left. No, I guess there's nobody got any better right to it than the kid. We'll inquire around and see. But seein' the gold is found on the claim, and we've got the claim according to law, looks to me like—"

"Well, here's your clean-up, old prospector. Don't swallow any, is all. let's weigh it out, Cash, and see how much it is, just for a josh."

Lovin Child had nuggets to play with there on the bed, and told the world many unintelligible things about it. Cash and Bud dumped all the gold into a pan, and weighed it out on the little scales Cash had for his tests. It was not a fortune, as fortunes go. It was probably all the gold Nelson had panned out in a couple of years, working alone and with crude devices. A little over twenty-three hundred dollars it amounted to, not counting the nuggets which Lovin Child had on the bunk with him.

"Well, it's a start for the kid, anyway," Bud said, leaning back and regarding the heap with eyes shining. "I helped him find it, and I kinda feel as if I'm square with him now for not giving him my half the claim. Twenty-three hundred would be a good price for a half interest, as the claims stand, don't yuh think, Cash?"

"Yeah—well, I dunno's I'd sell for that. But on the showing we've got so far— yes, five thousand, say, for the claims would be good money."

"Pretty good haul for a kid, anyway. He's got a couple of hundred dollars in nuggets, right there on the bunk. Let's see, Lovins. Let Bud have 'em for a minute."

Then it was that Lovin Child revealed a primitive human trait. He would not give up the gold. He held fast to one big nugget, spread his fat legs over the remaining heap of them, and fought Bud's hand away with the other fist.

"No, no, no! Tell a worl' no, no, no!" he remonstrated vehemently, until Bud whooped with laughter.

"All right—all right! Keep your gold, durn it. You're like all the rest—minute you get your paws on to some of the real stuff, you go hog-wild over it."

Cash was pouring the fine gold back into the buck skin bag and the baking-powder cans.

"Let the kid play with it," he said. "Getting used to gold when he's little will maybe save him from a lot of foolishness over it when he gets big. I dunno, but it looks reasonable to me. Let him have a few nuggets if he wants. Familiarity breeds contempt, they say; maybe he won't get to thinkin' too much of it if he's got it around under his nose all the time. Same as everything else. It's the finding that hits a feller hardest, Bud—the hunting for it and dreaming about it and not finding it. What say we go up to the claim for an hour or so? Take the kid along. It won't hurt him if he's bundled up good. It ain't cold to-day, anyhow."

That night they discussed soberly the prospects of the claim and their responsibilities in the matter of Lovin Child's windfall. They would quietly investigate the history of old Nelson, who had died a pauper in the eyes of the community, with all his gleanings of gold hidden away. They agreed that Lovin Child should not start off with one grain of gold that rightfully belonged to some one else—but they agreed the more cheerfully because neither man believed they would find any close relatives; a wife or children they decided upon as rightful heirs. Brothers, sisters, cousins, and aunts did not count. They were presumably able to look after themselves just as old Nelson had done. Their ethics were simple enough, surely.

Barring, then, the discovery of rightful heirs, their plan was to take the gold to Sacramento in the spring, and deposit it there in a savings bank for one Lovins Markham Moore. They would let the interest "ride" with the principal, and they would—though neither openly confessed it to the other—from time to time add a little from their own earnings. Bud especially looked forward to that as a compromise with his duty to his own child. He intended to save every cent he could, and to start a savings account in the same bank, for his own baby, Robert Edward Moore—named for Bud. He could not start off with as large a sum as Lovins would have, and for that Bud was honestly sorry. But Robert Edward Moore would have Bud's share in the claims, which would do a little toward evening things up.

Having settled these things to the satisfaction of their desires and their consciences, they went to bed well pleased with the day.

CHAPTER TWENTY-ONE.
MARIE'S SIDE OF IT

We all realize keenly, one time or another, the abject poverty of language. To attempt putting some emotions into words is like trying to play Ave Maria on a toy piano. There are heights and depths utterly beyond the limitation of instrument and speech alike.

Marie's agonized experience in Alpine—and afterward—was of that kind. She went there under the lure of her loneliness, her heart-hunger for Bud. Drunk or sober, loving her still or turning away in anger, she had to see him; had to hear him speak; had to tell him a little of what she felt of penitence and longing, for that is what she believed she had to do. Once she had started, she could not turn back. Come what might, she would hunt until she found him. She had to, or go crazy, she told herself over and over. She could not imagine any circumstance that would turn her back from that quest.

Yet she did turn back—and with scarce a thought of Bud. She could not imagine the thing happening that did happen, which is the way life has of keeping us all on the anxious seat most of the time. She could not—at least she did not—dream that Lovin Child, at once her comfort and her strongest argument for a new chance at happiness, would in ten minutes or so wipe out all thought of Bud and leave only a dumb, dreadful agony that hounded her day and night.

She had reached Alpine early in the forenoon, and had gone to the one little hotel, to rest and gather up her courage for the search which she felt was only beginning. She had been too careful of her money to spend any for a sleeper, foregoing even a berth in the tourist car. She could make Lovin Child comfortable with a full seat in the day coach for his little bed, and for herself it did not matter. She could not sleep anyway. So she sat up all night and thought, and worried over the future which was foolish, since the future held nothing at all that she pictured in it.

She was tired when she reached the hotel, carrying Lovin Child and her suit case too—porters being unheard of in small villages, and the one hotel being too sure of its patronage to bother about getting guests from depot to hall bedroom. A deaf old fellow with white whiskers and poor eyesight fumbled two or three keys on a nail, chose one and led the way down a little dark hall to a little, stuffy room with another door opening directly on the sidewalk. Marie had not registered on her arrival, because there was no ink in the inkwell, and the pen had only half a point; but she was rather relieved to find that she was not obliged to write her name down—for Bud, perhaps, to see before she had a chance to see him.

Lovin Child was in his most romping, rambunctious mood, and Marie's head ached so badly that she was not quite so watchful of his movements as usual. She gave him a cracker and left him alone to investigate the tiny room while she laid down for just a minute on the bed, grateful because the sun shone in warmly through the window and she did not feel the absence of a fire. She had no intention whatever of going to sleep—she did not believe that she could sleep if she had wanted to. Fall asleep she did, however, and she must have slept for at least half an hour, perhaps longer.

When she sat up with that startled sensation that follows unexpected, undesired slumber, the door was open, and Lovin Child was gone. She had not believed that he could open the door, but she discovered that its latch had a very precarious hold upon the worn facing, and that a slight twist of the knob was all it needed to swing the door open. She rushed out, of course, to look for him, though, unaware of how long she had slept, she was not greatly disturbed. Marie had run after Lovin Child too often to be alarmed at a little thing like that.

I don't know when fear first took hold of her, or when fear was swept away by the keen agony of loss. She went the whole length of the one little street, and looked in all the open doorways, and traversed the one short alley that led behind the hotel. Facing the street was the railroad, with the station farther up at the edge of the timber. Across the railroad was the little, rushing river, swollen now with rains that had been snow on the higher slopes of the mountain behind the town.

Marie did not go near the river at first. Some instinct of dread made her shun even the possibility that Lovin Child had headed that way. But a man told her, when she broke down her diffidence and inquired, that he had seen a little tot in a red suit and cap going off that way. He had not thought anything of it. He was a stranger himself, he said, and he supposed the kid belonged there, maybe.

Marie flew to the river, the man running beside her, and three or four others coming out of buildings to see what was the matter. She did not find Lovin Child, but she did find half of the cracker she had given him. It was lying so close to a deep, swirly place under the bank that Marie gave a scream when she saw it, and the man caught her by the arm for fear she meant to jump in.

Thereafter, the whole of Alpine turned out and searched the river bank as far down as they could get into the box canyon through which it roared to the sage-covered hills beyond. No one doubted that Lovin Child had been swept away in that tearing, rock-churned current. No one had any hope of finding his body, though they searched just as diligently as if they were certain.

Marie walked the bank all that day, calling and crying and fighting off despair. She walked the floor of her little room all night, the door locked against sympathy that seemed to her nothing but a prying curiosity over her torment, fighting back the hysterical cries that kept struggling for outlet.

The next day she was too exhausted to do anything more than climb up the steps of the train when it stopped there. Towns and ranches on the river below had been warned by wire and telephone and a dozen officious citizens of Alpine assured her over and over that she would be notified at once if anything was discovered; meaning, of course, the body of her child. She did not talk. Beyond telling the station agent her name, and that she was going to stay in Sacramento until she heard something, she shrank behind her silence and would reveal nothing of her errand there in Alpine, nothing whatever concerning herself. Mrs. Marie Moore, General Delivery, Sacramento, was all that Alpine learned of her.

It is not surprising then, that the subject was talked out long before Bud or Cash came down into the town more than two months later. It is not surprising, either, that no one thought to look up-stream for the baby, or that they failed to consider any possible fate for him save drowning. That nibbled piece of cracker on the very edge of the river threw them all off in their reasoning. They took it for granted that the baby had fallen into the river at the place where they found the cracker. If he had done so, he would have been swept away instantly. No one could look at the river and doubt that—therefore no one did doubt it. That a squaw should find him sitting down where he had fallen, two hundred yards above the town and in the edge of the thick timber, never entered their minds at all. That she should pick him up with the intention at first of stopping his crying, and should yield to the temptingness of him just as Bud had yielded, would have seemed to Alpine still more unlikely; because no Indian had ever kidnapped a white child in that neighborhood. So much for the habit of thinking along grooves established by precedent

Marie went to Sacramento merely because that was the closest town of any size, where she could wait for the news she dreaded to receive yet must receive before she could even begin to face her tragedy. She did not want to find Bud now. She shrank from any thought of him. Only for him, she would still have her Lovin Child. Illogically she blamed Bud for what had happened. He had caused her one more great heartache, and she hoped never to see him again or to hear his name spoken.

Dully she settled down in a cheap, semi-private boarding house to wait. In a day or two she pulled herself together and went out to look for work, because she must have money to live on. Go home to her mother she would not. Nor did she write to her. There, too, her great hurt had flung some of the blame. If her mother had not interfered and found fault all the time with Bud, they would be living together now—happy. It was her mother who had really brought about their separation. Her mother would nag at her now for going after Bud, would say that she deserved to lose her baby as a punishment for letting go her pride and self-respect. No, she certainly did not want to see her mother, or any one else she had ever known. Bud least of all.

She found work without much trouble, for she was neat and efficient looking, of the type that seems to belong in a well-ordered office, behind a typewriter desk near a window where the sun shines in. The place did not require much concentration—a dentist's office, where her chief duties consisted of opening the daily budget of circulars, sending out monthly bills, and telling pained-looking callers that the doctor was out just then. Her salary just about paid her board, with a dollar or two left over for headache tablets and a vaudeville show now and then. She did not need much spending money, for her evenings were spent mostly in crying over certain small garments and a canton-flannel dog called "Wooh-wooh."

For three months she stayed, too apathetic to seek a better position. Then the dentist's creditors became suddenly impatient, and the dentist could not pay his office rent, much less his office girl. Wherefore Marie found herself looking for work again, just when spring was opening all the fruit blossoms and merchants were smilingly telling one another that business was picking up.

Weinstock-Lubin's big department store gave her desk space in the mail-order department. Marie's duty it was to open the mail, check up the orders, and see that enough money was sent, and start the wheels moving to fill each order—to the satisfaction of the customer if possible.

At first the work worried her a little. But she became accustomed to it, and settled into the routine of passing the orders along the proper channels with as little individual thought given to each one as was compatible with efficiency. She became acquainted with some of the girls, and changed to a better boarding house. She still cried over the wooh-wooh and the little garments, but she did not cry so often, nor did she buy so many headache tablets. She was learning the futility of grief and the wisdom of turning her back upon sorrow when she could. The sight of a two-year-old baby boy would still bring tears to her eyes, and she could not sit through a picture show that had scenes of children and happy married couples, but she fought the pain of it as a weakness which she must overcome. Her Lovin Child was gone; she had given up everything but the sweet, poignant memory of how pretty he had been and how endearing.

Then, one morning in early June, her practiced fingers were going through the pile of mail orders and they singled out one that carried the postmark of Alpine. Marie bit her lips, but her fingers did not falter in their task. Cheap table linen, cheap collars, cheap suits or cheap something-or-other was wanted, she had no doubt. She took out the paper with the blue money order folded inside, speared the money order on the hook with others, drew her order pad closer, and began to go through the list of articles wanted.

This was the list:—

XL	94,	3	Dig in the mud suits, 3 yr at 59c	$1.77
XL	14	1	Buddy tucker suit 3 yr	2.00
KL	6	1	Bunny pumps infant 5	1.25
KL	54	1	Fat Ankle shoe infant 5	.98
HL	389	4	Rubens vests, 3 yr at 90c	2.70
SL	418	3	Pajamas 3 yr. at 59c	1.77
OL	823	1	Express wagon, 15x32 in.	4.25

$14.22

For which money order is enclosed. Please ship at once.

Very truly,
R. E. MOORE,
Alpine, Calif.

Mechanically she copied the order on a slip of paper which she put into her pocket, left her desk and her work and the store, and hurried to her boarding house.

Not until she was in her own room with the door locked did she dare let herself think. She sat down with the copy spread open before her, her slim fingers pressing against her temples. Something amazing had been revealed to her—something so amazing that she could scarcely comprehend its full significance. Bud—never for a minute did she doubt that it was Bud, for she knew his handwriting too well to be mistaken—Bud was sending for clothes for a baby boy!

"3 Dig in the mud suits, 3 yr—" it sounded, to the hungry mother soul of her, exactly like her Lovin Child. She could see so vividly just how he would look in them. And the size—she certainly would buy than three-year size, if she were buying for Lovin Child. And the little "Buddy tucker" suit—that, too, sounded like Lovin Child. He must—Bud certainly must have him up there with him! Then Lovin Child was not drowned at all, but alive and needing dig-in-the-muds.

"Bud's got him! Oh, Bud has got him, I know he's got him!" she whispered over and over to herself in an ecstasy of hope. "My little Lovin Man! He's up there right now with his Daddy Bud—"

A vague anger stirred faintly, flared, died almost, flared again and burned steadily within her. Bud had her Lovin Child! How did he come to have him, then, unless he stole him? Stole him away, and let her suffer all this while, believing her baby was dead in the river!

"You devil!" she muttered, gritting her teeth when that thought formed clearly in her mind. "Oh, you devil, you! If you think you can get away with a thing like that—You devil!"

CHAPTER TWENTY-TWO.
THE CURE COMPLETE

In Nelson Flat the lupines were like spilled bluing in great, acre-wide blots upon the meadow grass. Between cabin and creek bank a little plot had been spaded and raked smooth, and already the peas and lettuce and radishes were up and growing as if they knew how short would be the season, and meant to take advantage of every minute of the warm days. Here and there certain plants were lifting themselves all awry from where they had been pressed flat by two small feet that had strutted heedlessly down the rows.

The cabin yard was clean, and the two small windows were curtained with cheap, white scrim. All before the door and on the path to the creek small footprints were scattered thick. It was these that Marie pulled up her hired saddle horse to study in hot resentment.

"The big brute!" she gritted, and got off and went to the cabin door, walking straight-backed and every mental and physical fiber of her braced for the coming struggle. She even regretted not having a gun; rather, she wished that she was not more afraid of a gun than of any possible need of one. She felt, at that minute, as though she could shoot Bud Moore with no more compunction that she would feel in swatting a fly.

That the cabin was empty and unlocked only made her blood boil the hotter. She went in and looked around at the crude furnishings and the small personal belongings of those who lived there. She saw the table all set ready for the next meal, with the extremely rustic high-chair that had DYNAMITE painted boldly on the side of the box seat. Fastened to a nail at one side of the box was a belt, evidently kept there for the purpose of strapping a particularly wriggly young person into the chair. That smacked strongly of Lovin Child, sure enough. Marie remembered the various devices by which she had kept him in his go cart.

She went closer and inspected the belt indignantly. Just as she expected—it was Bud's belt; his old belt that she bought for him just after they were married. She supposed that box beside the queer high chair was where he would sit at table and stuff her baby with all kinds of things he shouldn't eat. Where was her baby? A fresh spasm of longing for Lovin Child drove her from the cabin. Find him she would, and that no matter how cunningly Bud had hidden him away.

On a rope stretched between a young cottonwood tree in full leaf and a scaly, red-barked cedar, clothes that had been washed were flapping lazily in the little breeze. Marie stopped and looked at them. A man's shirt and drawers, two towels gray for want of bluing, a little shirt and a nightgown and pair of stockings—and, directly in front of Marie, a small pair of blue overalls trimmed with red bands, the blue showing white fiber where the color had been scrubbed out of the cloth, the two knees flaunting patches sewed with long irregular stitches such as a man would take.

Bud and Lovin Child. As in the cabin, so here she felt the individuality in their belongings. Last night she had been tormented with the fear that there might be a wife as well as a baby boy in Bud's household. Even the evidence of the mail order, that held nothing for a woman and that was written by Bud's hand, could scarcely reassure her. Now she knew beyond all doubt that she had no woman to reckon with, and the knowledge brought relief of a sort.

She went up and touched the little overalls wistfully, laid her cheek against one little patch, ducked under the line, and followed a crooked little path that led up the creek. She forgot all about her horse, which looked after her as long as she was in sight, and then turned and trotted back the way it had come, wondering, no doubt, at the foolish faith this rider had in him.

The path led up along the side of the flat, through tall grass and all the brilliant blossoms of a mountain meadow in June. Great, graceful mountain lilies nodded from little shady tangles in the bushes. Harebells and lupines, wild-pea vines and columbines, tiny, gnome-faced pansies, violets, and the daintier flowering grasses lined the way with odorous loveliness. Birds called happily from the tree tops. Away up next the clouds an eagle sailed serene, alone, a tiny boat breasting the currents of the sky ocean.

Marie's rage cooled a little on that walk. It was so beautiful for Lovin Child, up here in this little valley among the snow-topped mountains; so sheltered. Yesterday's grind in that beehive of a department store seemed more remote than South Africa. Unconsciously her first nervous pace slackened. She found herself taking long breaths of this clean air, sweetened with the scent of growing things. Why couldn't the world be happy, since it was so beautiful? It made her think of those three weeks in Big Basin, and the never-forgettable wonder of their love—hers and Bud's.

She was crying with the pain and the beauty of it when she heard the first high, chirpy notes of a baby—her baby. Lovin Child was picketed to a young cedar near the mouth of the Blind ledge tunnel, and he was throwing rocks at a chipmunk that kept coming toward him in little rushes, hoping with each rush to get a crumb of the bread and butter that Lovin Child had flung down. Lovin Child was squealing and jabbering, with now and then a real word that he had learned from Bud and Cash. Not particularly nice words—"Doggone" was one and several times he called the chipmunk a "sunny-gun." And of course he frequently announced that he would "Tell a worl'" something. His head was bare and shone in the sun like the gold for which Cash and his Daddy Bud were digging, away back in the dark hole. He had on a pair of faded overalls trimmed with red, mates of the ones on the rope line, and he threw rocks impartially with first his right hand and then his left, and sometimes with both at once; which did not greatly distress the chipmunk, who knew Lovin Child of old and had learned how wide the rocks always went of their mark.

Upon this scene Marie came, still crying. She had always been an impulsive young woman, and now she forgot that Lovin Child had not seen her for six months or so, and that baby memories are short. She rushed in and snatched him off the ground and kissed him and squeezed him and cried aloud upon her God and her baby, and buried her wet face against his fat little neck.

Cash, trundling a wheelbarrow of ore out to the tunnel's mouth, heard a howl and broke into a run with his load, bursting out into the sunlight with a clatter and upsetting the barrow ten feet short of the regular dumping place. Marie was frantically trying to untie the rope, and was having trouble because Lovin Child was in one of his worst kicking-and-squirming tantrums. Cash rushed in and snatched the child from her.

"Here! What you doing to that kid? You're scaring him to death—and you've got no right!"

"I have got a right! I have too got a right!" Marie was clawing like a wildcat at Cash's grimy hands. "He's my baby! He's mine! You ought to be hung for stealing him away from me. Let go—he's mine, I tell you. Lovin! Lovin Child! Don't you know Marie? Marie's sweet, pitty man, he is! Come to Marie, boy baby!"

"Tell a worl' no, no, no!" yelled Lovin Child, clinging to Cash.

"Aw—come to Marie, sweetheart! Marie's own lovin' little man baby! You let him go, or I'll—I'll kill you. You big brute!"

Cash let go, but it was not because she commanded. He let go and stared hard at Marie, lifting his eyebrows comically as he stepped back, his hand going unconsciously up to smooth his beard.

"Marie?" he repeated stupidly. "Marie?" He reached out and laid a hand compellingly on her shoulder. "Ain't your name Marie Markham, young lady? Don't you know your own dad?"

Marie lifted her face from kissing Lovin Child very much against his will, and stared round-eyed at Cash. She did not say anything.

"You're my Marie, all right You ain't changed so much I can't recognize yuh. I should think you'd remember your own father—but I guess maybe the beard kinda changes my looks. Is this true, that this kid belongs to you?"

Marie gasped. "Why—father? Why—why, father!" She leaned herself and Lovin Child into his arms. "Why, I can't believe it! Why—" She closed her eyes and shivered, going suddenly weak, and relaxed in his arms. "I-I-I can't—"

Cash slid Lovin Child to the ground, where that young gentleman picked himself up indignantly and ran as far as his picket rope would let him, whereupon he turned and screamed "Sunny-gun! sunny-gun!" at the two like an enraged bluejay. Cash did not pay any attention to him. He was busy seeking out a soft, shady spot that was free of rocks, where he might lay Marie down. He leaned over her and fanned her violently with his hat, his lips and his eyebrows working with the complexity of his emotions. Then suddenly he turned and ducked into the tunnel, after Bud.

Bud heard him coming and turned from his work. Cash was not trundling the empty barrow, which in itself was proof enough that something had happened, even if Cash had not been running. Bud dropped his pick and started on a run to meet him.

"What's wrong? Is the kid—?"

"Kid's all right" Cash stopped abruptly, blocking Bud's way. "It's something else. Bud, his mother's come after him. She's out there now—laid out in a faint."

"Lemme go." Bud's voice had a grimness in it that spelled trouble for the lady laid out in a faint "She can be his mother a thousand times—"

"Yeah. Hold on a minute, Bud. You ain't going out there and raise no hell with that poor girl. Lovins belongs to her, and she's going to have him.... Now, just keep your shirt on a second. I've got something more to say. He's her kid, and she wants him back, and she's going to have him back. If you git him away from her, it'll be over my carcass. Now, now, hold on! H-o-l-d on! You're goin' up against Cash Markham now, remember! That girl is my girl! My girl that I ain't seen since she was a kid in short dresses. It's her father you've got to deal with now—her father and the kid's grandfather. You get that? You be reasonable, Bud, and there won't be no trouble at all. But my girl ain't goin' to be robbed of her baby—not whilst I'm around. You get that settled in your mind before you go out there, or—you don't go out whilst I'm here to stop you."

"You go to hell," Bud stated evenly, and thrust Cash aside with one sweep of his arm, and went down the tunnel. Cash, his eyebrows lifted with worry and alarm, was at his heels all the way.

"Now, Bud, be calm!" he adjured as he ran. "Don't go and make a dang fool of yourself! She's my girl, remember. You want to hold on to yourself, Bud, and be reasonable. Don't go and let your temper—"

"Shut your damn mouth!" Bud commanded him savagely, and went on running.

At the tunnel mouth he stopped and blinked, blinded for a moment by the strong sunlight in his face. Cash stumbled and lost ten seconds or so, picking himself up. Behind him Bud heard Cash panting, "Now, Bud, don't go and make—a dang fool—" Bud snorted contemptuously and leaped the dirt pile, landing close to Marie, who was just then raising herself dizzily to an elbow.

"Now, Bud," Cash called tardily when he had caught up with him, "you leave that girl alone! Don't you lay a finger on her! That's my—"

Bud lifted his lips away from Marie's and spoke over his shoulder, his arms tightening in their hold upon Marie's trembling, yielding body.

"Shut up, Cash. She's my wife—now where do you get off at?"

(That, o course, lacked a little of being the exact truth. Lacked a few hours, in fact, because they did not reach Alpine and the railroad until that afternoon, and were not remarried until seven o'clock that evening.)

"No, no, no!" cried Lovin Child from a safe distance. "Tell a worl' no, no!"

"I'll tell the world yes, yes!" Bud retorted ecstatically, lifting his face again. "Come here, you little scallywag, and love your mamma Marie. Cash, you old donkey, don't you get it yet? We've got 'em both for keeps, you and me."

"Yeah—I get it, all right." Cash came and stood awkwardly over them. "I get it—found my girl one minute, and lost her again the next! But I'll tell yeh one thing, Bud Moore. The kid's' goin' to call me grampaw, er I'll know the reason why!"

Lector House believes that a society develops through a two-fold approach of continuous learning and adaptation, which is derived from the study of classic literary works spread across the historic timeline of literature records. Therefore, we aim at reviving, repairing and redeveloping all those inaccessible or damaged but historically as well as culturally important literature across subjects so that the future generations may have an opportunity to study and learn from past works to embark upon a journey of creating a better future.

This book is a result of an effort made by Lector House towards making a contribution to the preservation and repair of original ancient works which might hold historical significance to the approach of continuous learning across subjects.

HAPPY READING & LEARNING!

LECTOR HOUSE LLP
E-MAIL: lectorpublishing@gmail.com